ADVANCE PRAISE

"*Racing Shadows* races literally between life and death, around plot curves and down fast-paced straightaways that will take your breath away. Jim Dill knows the terrain of the elite distance runner. Artfully he captures the rhythms of that world, all the dedication and sacrifices needed to run like few others."

— David L. Robbins, author of *War of the Rats* and *The Low Bird*.

"*Racing Shadows* explores how inner fears and insecurities from past events can haunt runners in the present, and how striving for a new goal can help in letting go and finding peace. Jeff Dillon and his coach search the origins of their disquiet and discover their journey together is about more than running, and that neither would find the peace they seek without the other. James Dill's own Olympic Marathon Trials experience and running journey bring reality to his prose and authenticity to the relationship between runner and coach."

— Dennis Barker, author of *The River Road*

"In *Racing Shadows*, James Dill's new novel about finishing life's toughest races, Dill takes readers on the literary equivalent of a fast-paced tempo run, moving more like a seasoned pro than a first-time author through a story of friendship, dedication, loss and victory. Dill doles out reader endorphins through deft racing scenes, around dark corners of his characters' pasts, and amidst the iconic running world of the competitive athlete. The pairing of odd couple distance runners – proven Bill and promising Jeff – isn't as unlikely as it is extraordinary. The two set out to exorcise old demons – lost loves, lost races and selves – and find in each other a once-in-a-lifetime friendship not of this world. Dill, a 1984 Olympic marathon hopeful, writes from a place deep within every runner aiming to defy physical limitations to rank as a world-class elite, wondering from where the required super human strength will come and finding it only when they look to something bigger than themselves. Readers will love *Racing Shadows,* an intimate story of love and friendship that reveals the expansiveness of the human spirit, arriving at the finish winded but ready for more."

— Joni Albrecht, Editor, *Little Star*

"*Racing Shadows* is a compelling story that delves into the heart, mind and soul of a dedicated distance runner aiming to reach his athletic potential while struggling to balance personal relationships, school and training. An added twist is his unlikely coach who takes us on a pathway never imagined. Whether you raced during the running boom or wonder what it was like to have been racing in the late 1970s and early 1980s, you will not be able to put this book down once you start reading. *Racing Shadows* took me on a journey different from that in any of the hundreds of books and articles I have read on the sport of running and is immensely satisfying."

— Gary Cohen is founder of garycohenrunning.com and his over 125 monthly interviews include more than 70 Olympians. He is one of less than 30 persons worldwide to ever race a sub-3:00 marathon in five decades with a best time of 2:22:34.

Racing Shadows

Racing Shadows

a novel

Lance
Happy running.

James K. Dill

[signature]

Apprentice
House Press
Loyola University Maryland

Note: This book is a work of fiction. The characters are fictional; amalgams of people, events from the past, and my imagination during the many miles run. Certain sports figures and their actual races are included for historical accuracy.

First Edition

Casebound ISBN: 978-1-62720-241-1
Paperback ISBN: 978-1-62720-242-8
Ebook ISBN: 978-1-62720-243-5

Printed in the United States of America

Design by Molly Werts
Editorial development by Cara Hullings
Promotion plan development by Miranda Nolan

Photo of Bill Agee on page 178 used by permission of *The Baltimore Sun*

Published by Apprentice House Press

Apprentice
House Press
Loyola University Maryland

Apprentice House Press
Loyola University Maryland
4501 N. Charles Street
Baltimore, MD 21210
410.617.5265 • 410.617.2198 (fax)
www.ApprenticeHouse.com
info@ApprenticeHouse.com

For Wendy, a runner's wife, and now a writer's wife. Among your many charms, I'm grateful for your patience.

And Dad, for all you've given me.

"Men, today we die a little."

—Emile Zatopek, Gold Medalist, prior to the start
of the 1956 Olympic Marathon

*"The credit belongs to the man who is actually in the arena, whose face is
marred by dust and sweat and blood, who strives valiantly; who errs, who
comes short again and again..."*

—Theodore Roosevelt

CHAPTER I

May 26, 1984, Buffalo, New York

"He needs my help." Bill spoke to no one in particular. No one paid him any attention with what was happening on the street below. He stood apart from the crowd in a dated raincoat and a wide-brimmed hat; a contrast to the competitors that dashed by in their bright, nylon running gear. Bill watched the random activity of the competitors. "Days like this were full of promise." He closed his eyes and breathed in deeply to smell the fresh cut grass warmed by the sun. "I lived for days like this one. Finish the chores, a cup of tea and a biscuit before heading off to race. Run hard, then pats on the back and pints at the pub." The day smelled like boyhood. A picture of simpler times crossed his mind. Bill stood in the shadow of the Albright-Knox Gallery; the iconic, hundred-year old structure loomed over the park and the start of the race. "Only thing older than me around here." He chuckled, patting one of the Greek columns.

He was there to watch Jeff Dillon, busy warming up for the race. Jeff wore bib number 163. A good runner, a qualifier, but not one of the favorites. In Bill's day he would have been known as a journeyman, recruited by the club to help win the team trophy. Jeff was taller and more muscular than many of the other competitors. He wore navy shorts and a red and white mesh top. The young man shook his shaggy blond hair. Bill laughed; the hairstyles had changed since his day.

He hoped the boy would have a good day. Racing in the U.S. Olympic Marathon Trials was a heady experience. The race was the pinnacle of his sport and only occurred once every four years. It would be a hard race, likely a fast, steady pace from the start. Anyone not ready would be left behind. Bill knew the marathon well; she could be cruel. Win or lose, he'd meet the boy today, having waited long enough. Bill pulled his hat low to shade his eyes and walked down the hill towards the start and Jeff. As he walked, he admitted to himself that maybe, he needed the boy, too.

****

Jeff jogged to the porta-potty for a last nervous pee. He wanted no distractions mid-race. After nature's call, he picked a final cup of water from the competitor's table to moisten his dry, cottony mouth. A couple of sips made it down, the rest he swished and spit into the grass. Hydration would be critical with two hours of work ahead, the day already warm and humid. There was no breeze. Jeff's heart fluttered from coffee, adrenaline, and the thrill of running with the fastest men on the planet.

He sat on the curb to strip off his warm-up gear. Alberto Salazar, the favorite and world record holder, sat next to him, intent on the same task. Jeff glanced at the legend furtively; all muscle and bone, just like Jeff. Alberto would run his miles at sub-5-minute pace today versus Jeff's 5:10 to 5:20 per mile pace. That small difference in pace would add up by the finish. His stargazing was interrupted by a young boy, asking for an autograph. The boy held out a program and pen.

"Go ahead, son. Ask him," the father urged.

"Who are you? Will you win the race?" He pronounced it, 'wace.'

"I'm, Jeff Dillon, from North Carolina. I don't know if I'll win today, but I'll give it my best. What's your name?"

"Wob," he said.

"Do you like to run, Rob?" The boy nodded, then sprinted a few steps across the road and back, demonstrating his form. "That's how I started. I liked to run on the playground. Keep it up and you'll be here one day."

Jeff took the pen and signed the program. He then posed for a photo and pinned his sponsor's commemorative pin on the boy's shirt.

"Here you go, your first medal." The boy beamed.

Jeff said goodbye, looking to Salazar but he'd seen his chance and darted off. Jeff shrugged and patted the boy's head.

"Gotta go." He checked the double knots on his shoes and decided he was ready. It had all come down to this one race. The playground, junior high and high school cross country, college track. The training and racing; miles and miles of asphalt that passed under his trainers. The goal had always been to race at the championship level. He'd finally made it fourteen years after he'd taken that first run. He would race in the U.S. Olympic Trials.

Jeff's manager, Ken, walked up with his teammates Wally, and Rick. They looked just as wired as Jeff.

"Hey, guys." He shook Ken's hand and nodded to the other two.

"You ready, Jeff?" Ken asked.

"I'm so nervous, I feel like I'm vibrating." His hands shook.

"Frog on a hotplate?" Rick asked.

"Yep."

"Cat on a hot tin roof?"

"Yep."

"Chicken on a conveyor belt at the processing plant?"

"Yeah." They laughed at the gallows humor. His mouth went dry again.

"Look, guys. Enjoy this." Ken pulled them into a huddle. "This isn't New York or Boston with ten thousand hobby-joggers. You're at the Olympic Trials and only two hundred qualified. You're in elite company and at the top of your sport. Converse is proud of you and happy to have you here competing in their gear. Just run your race and try not let the pressure get to you. You each know what sort of race to run. Put all that training to work and have a good day. I have your gear. We'll have a tent and some cold Canadian beverages at the finish." Ken's words struck home. A former Olympian at 800-meters, he'd stood where they stood, staring down the task ahead.

Jeff jogged to the start in a fog. Nervous sweat dripped down his arms and torso. He found a spot near the middle of the pack, ten yards back from the actual line. His strategy was to work his way up during the 26-miles to

3

finish in the top twenty. Rogers, Durden, Mathews, Pfitzinger, and Salazar, the favorites, jostled for the front line up ahead. They could have it and their sub-five pace. All Jeff wanted was a controlled effort and a top finish.

Alone in the pack, Jeff tried not to dwell on the task ahead; racing twenty-six miles faster than he ever had. It was daunting. The runners would race the first five miles through the streets of Buffalo before crossing into Ontario, Canada, for the final 21-miles along the Niagara Parkway and the sprint to the finish at the famous Falls. He took in as much warm, sweat-tinged air through his nostrils as he could. They flared with the effort. The quarters were close, bodies all around, he stared at the small patch of pavement between his shoes.

After too many introductions and a long National Anthem, the runners were called to their places and set. The military cannon sounded from the hill. Jeff felt the concussion and took his first steps. The pack moved slowly at first, expanding accordion-like in the street. Jeff crossed the wavy red, white, and blue starting line, his speed building, the race had begun. One hundred and sixty men, reduced from the two hundred plus qualifiers raced through the streets of Buffalo.

The first mile went by in 5-minutes and 15-seconds, a pace that normally felt fairly easy. This felt much faster. Jeff positioned himself in the middle of the pack to help pull him along. His respiration seemed faster than normal. "Relax," he told himself, "it's normal, your first National Championship."

Jeff ran in the second pack, sixty strong and very compact. There was little room to stride out, his elbows and knees constrained by those around him. He moved toward the curb for more room. Losing a shoe or taking a tumble was something he could not afford. The first water station came up at two miles. Jeff grabbed a cup of water. He took small sips while negotiating the discarded cups and bottles dropped by the leaders. He poured the last sip on his head to cool the fever.

They'd navigated downtown. The towers of the Peace Bridge appeared above the tree line ahead. The large group ran up the metal grate, towards the five-mile mark. The slight hill felt good after the flat pavement. Jeff watched the leaders snake off the front of the bridge ahead of him. Wilson, a friend from Northern Virginia had taken the lead. A race helicopter zoomed from underneath the bridge, startling him with the blast from its rotors. It buzzed quickly ahead to catch the front pack.

Jeff's group reached the Niagara Parkway and the promise of shade, a river breeze, and the long, flat roadway. The shade and breeze were a myth. He had only the relentless pace and asphalt. His pack had decreased to thirty or so, the others dropping back in ones and two's. Jeff passed the 10-mile mark in 52-minutes, 2:16 finish pace and his goal. If he maintained, he'd likely finish in the top 20 and receive a high ranking. There was a glimmer of hope along with a growing sense of unease.

Jeff came up on Rick. "Looking good, buddy. Getting any easier?"

He shook his head no, focused on the road.

"Me either." Their paths parted at the next aid station. He hadn't seen Wally, the fastest of the three. He'd be somewhere up ahead.

Jeff reached 13-miles and the halfway point in 1-hour, 9-minutes. His pace had slowed slightly, but still a sub-2:20 finish. He'd take that result. The unsettled feeling that had dogged him the last few miles had transformed to numbness. It crept into his extremities, chewing at his form.

Jeff's passed 15-miles, coaching himself that there was just a little over 10-miles remaining. He could do it. Needing refreshment, he grabbed a cup from the table. It wasn't water but Gatorade. He usually bypassed the sports drink but the salty-sweet liquid tasted wonderful. Despite the refreshment, a dull ache radiated from his arms, legs, and torso. The pavement had become a boxer; its body blows irreversible. The Gatorade came back up without warning. A bright yellow mass spewed from his mouth to splatter on the side of the road. A spectator in his peripheral vision jumped to avoid the neon liquid.

Jeff hoped he'd feel better with his stomach empty. He'd rallied at Milwaukee, the last six miles his fastest of the race. But Buffalo was not Milwaukee. His mouth filled with bile. He spat the acid to the street and wiped his mouth with his hand. There would be no miracles finishes this day. He stopped at the next aid station and paused to drink a full cup of water and rinse his mouth. He stopped because he had to despite knowing the physics principle that also applied to road racing; *a body in motion stays in motion, a body at rest stays at rest.* Rarely did a runner at this level stop and regain his pace. His energy reserves were depleted and the muscle cells in his legs shattered. Sadness at the outcome of his race competed with relief to be finished. The pain began to ebb for the first time that day.

Jeff walked a few steps before jogging slowly, continuing towards the finish. Those who had fallen behind earlier now moved past in their own tortured pace. Some offered a quiet, "good job" or fanny pat, to urge him to finish. Rick jogged past, his day over, too.

"You can do it, Dillon. Finish line's not far."

The disappointment of his race covered him like the sweat that poured off his body. He had vomited his boyhood dream onto the side of the road in one colorful splash. There were no answers to the many questions that plagued him, his painful walk-jog to the finish took his full concentration. One day, this would be just another race that hadn't gone well. He knew he'd have better days and race again, but that didn't help at the moment, his dream deflated. Jogging slowly, the reality of the hundreds of miles and years of training and sacrifice sunk in. It would be another four years until the next Trials, and that was too much to think about.

Jeff spotted the twenty six-mile marker with relief. He had only a couple of hundred yards to go. The Skylon Observation Tower rose out of the mist ahead, alien to the landscape. With the finish line banner in sight, a different sound rose above the roar of the crowd, announcer, and the falls. It was a sound he'd never heard before. The race had decided she was not through with him. There would be one last insult. The meat wagon, the ambulance that followed the last runner home, crept behind Jeff like the Grim Reaper. He would finish last.

The digital clock flashed his results, 2-hours, 37-minutes, number 108. Jeff lurched across the line. He bent over, hands on his knees in the familiar post-race recovery position. It felt good to stop. He stood alone in the shoot. Helpers moved him in a crab-like walk and someone asked if he needed medical attention. He waved them off.

A pair of shoes appeared in the grass before him. They were worn, two-tone wingtips. A weathered hand appeared. "The name's Bill, Bill Atlee."

Jeff tried to stand, his legs shakey. Bill wore light colored pants, a bulky raincoat, and held a wide-brimmed hat. He had thick, white hair and brown eyes that squinted through wrinkles on a well-worn face. His smile was broad.

"Had a rough day, did you, my boy? I wouldn't be too hard on yourself. Your time today was the same as mine when I won the 1928 Trials in Baltimore. What are the chances that we would run the same time, fifty-four years apart?" He chuckled.

"Who are you?" Jeff muttered, still breathing hard. He straightened to his full height, a full head taller than Bill. His head throbbed, his chest heaved. Too unstable, he let the old man assist him, his grip surprisingly strong and cold. Jeff shivered from the breeze that bubbled up from the falls, cool for the first time that day. Goosebumps ran down his arms and back.

"Come on lad. Let's walk so you don't tie up. You need to drink, too. Something not so yellow. You almost got me back at sixteen." He chuckled again. They stopped at a deserted bench on the edge of the crowd.

Jeff took a second look at Bill. It seemed odd that he could have been at sixteen and here at the finish with no vehicles allowed on the course.

"I caught a ride on the press truck." Bill replied as if he read Jeff's thoughts.

Jeff sipped a cup of water, sitting on the bench while Bill stood. He rocked on his heels with his hands in the pockets of the big coat. The water roared behind him, making it hard to hear.

"Jeffrey," he began. "You will shake this off. Don't be too hard on yourself. You'll live to fight another day. As Teddy Roosevelt once said, *'you were the man in the arena. The man who took all the chances and worked hard. Work others will never know.'* What's important is that you qualified and you raced. No one will ever know what you went through out there today or what it took for you to get here. But you and I know and that's something."

Jeff didn't get everything the old man said, something about Teddy and an arena. "Look, I don't know if there will be another race. This one hurt worse than anything I've ever felt, and I don't think I can face that kind of pain and disappointment again."

"Well, it's not a day for answers. Just recover. You and I will talk again."

"Talk again? I don't know you. I mean it's cool to meet you, and I am impressed you won the trials, when did you say?

"It was in 1928, in Baltimore for the Amsterdam Games that year."

"I doubt I'll ever be in Buffalo again."

"Oh, I'm sorry, Jeffrey. Didn't I mention I live near you in North Carolina? I introduced myself so we can be acquaintances and friends perhaps. I've followed your career for a while now. Call me a fan." He laughed easily. "If you don't mind me saying so, it appears you could use someone to advise you. Would you like to work together? We would do so on your terms, of course."

Jeff didn't know what to say. The old bird had appeared out of nowhere and seemed to know him. He also knew he needed a coach, something he had sought and something Ken had advised him to arrange. A former Olympian to help coach him might be the silver lining of the long, disastrous day. Jeff looked for Bill, but he had left. Ken strode toward the bench.

"Hey, Jeff, what are you doing way over here? I've been looking all over the finish for you. How are you feeling?" He didn't wait for Jeff to answer. "I'm sorry you didn't have a better day. If it makes you feel any better, neither did Wally or Rick, but that's the marathon game. Let's get your gear. The other guys are over at the tent. We can talk on the way to the airport." Jeff took a hand from his manager, his legs wobbly like a newborn colt. Apparently, Bill had lost interest and gone somewhere else. Jeff walked gingerly, blood spots on his shoes showed where his blisters had popped. He struggled to walk, his large leg muscles had tightened up significantly. At the team tent, he gratefully pulled an icy, Molson Ale from the cooler. His Olympic Trials were officially over, the cold beer and having finished his reward for the day.

****

Bill watched the two men walk away. He'd accomplished what he came to do; introduce himself to the young marathoner. The boy had talent, but he needed guidance and a proper coach. It would be delicate after today's performance, but he was young and would recover. The boy also needed to eliminate the distractions from his life. With a little focus and confidence, he could be good, even great.

Bill sighed and pulled his hat low in the draft and mist that whipped up from the falls. The post race festivities were underway: speeches, the medal ceremony, and a band played somewhere nearby. A helicopter zipped just above the trees. In his day it would have been a Zeppelin. The thought made him laugh, a Zeppelin bouncing around in the breezes above the falls like a dark cloud. Bill walked away from the festivities into the mist.

****

The ride to the airport was long and quiet, traveling the same parkway he had just raced seemed cruel. Jeff sipped another Molson in silence, watching the Canadian countryside pass and the bridge that signified the U.S. border loom ahead. He wanted only to get to the airport, fly home, and sleep.

"Don't worry about today, Jeff. You've shown your ability and represented us well the past couple of years. You're our best marathoner in the Carolina's. Just pick out your next race later this year and I'll come down to support you. I'm sure you'll make the podium next time."

"I have no idea where I'll race next. I'm pretty depressed about the whole running thing right now."

"Don't think about it, not right now. Get back to Winston-Salem and recover. Take some time off and plan your fall training. Consider a late fall or winter race. I also think you need to find a coach, someone to oversee your work and help with race strategy. I can help find someone if there's no one available locally."

"A coach would help. I talked to a guy at the finish today from Winston-Salem. It was strange because he offered to help me. I'll tell you more about him once we talk."

Jeff understood his manager. He 'needed' to make the podium at the next race to maintain his sponsorship. He had one more chance, or he'd be on his own, struggling to buy good equipment, paying his own way to race, just another runner at the start of the race, sub-elite. The pressure of sponsorship and the after-effects of the race were a double-whammy. Depression swirled just below the surface. He closed his eyes and hoped the airport would be in sight when he opened them.

****

Jeff switched flights in Cincinnati. He also switched from beer to Jim Beam. Three of the miniatures lined his seatback tray.

He dozed, replaying his failure in the race he'd always dreamed of running, but the finishing position didn't change. How was that possible? He'd never been last in his life. Granted, it was a fast field, each competitor at least as fast as the other, and someone had to finish last, but why him? Pondering his failure, he thought of his father, who would be expecting a call. That call would have to wait. It was difficult to talk to the man, a success in life, in business, and in his 26-year marriage to Jeff's mother. Twenty-six; the number haunted him, the years of marriage for his parents and the miles he had failed to race that day.

"Can I take those, sir?" The flight attendant leaned over to take the little bottles. Jeff returned from his thoughts. He splashed the contents of the last bottle over what remained of the ice cubes.

"Sure, I'm finished."

"Are you an athlete?" She hovered over him, his warm-up gear and trainers noticeable.

"Oh, yeah, I am, or at least, I was. I ran in the Olympic Trials today."

"Did you win?"

The absurdity of her question struck him and he wanted to laugh, but how would she know. "Thank you, no. I didn't win. I finished last, and that may be my legacy."

Her bright smile turned into a frown. She murmured a quick, "I'm sorry," and scuttled off. Jeff turned back to the window and sipped the amber liquid, enjoying the warm sensation that helped mask his pain.

****

"There you are." Libby stood in front of him. "You're at the wrong terminal. How'd you get here?"

"I have no idea."

"I do, and his name is Jim Beam," she sniffed. "Come on, let's get you home and you can tell me all about it. It doesn't sound good."

Jeff clung to Libby. She loaded him into her car and drove back to his apartment. She stripped him of his sweats and running gear, the numbers still pinned to his singlet. She dropped everything in the hamper while he sat listlessly on the bed.

"I failed," was all he could manage. Libby guided him into the shower, his head down. After a few minutes under the hot water, she coaxed him out and dried him. It wasn't easy with his inebriated state and their height difference. She rolled him into bed, turned out the light, and climbed in beside him.

CHAPTER 2

May 27, 1984, Winston-Salem, North Carolina

Jeff stretched painfully; the muscles in his back and legs had cramped during the night. He rolled over with some difficulty in the waterbed, greeted by the very desirable derrière of Libby, his classmate and more. She stood beside the bed, drying her hair with a towel, unaware he was watching. He enjoyed the view, her curves enhanced by the small movements of her body.

"The view's so nice, and the bed so warm," he murmured. "I may not get up today." The damp towel hit him in the face.

"I wish I could stay with you, but I can't. I have work, perv. You should rest today and take it easy this week. You've been through a lot." She slipped on her underclothes, pulled on shorts, and a light blue tank top. The shirt's color matched her eyes and featured a pissed-off Tweety-Bird. The caricature was fitting; the little bird with the big head scowled with its tiny wings on its hips. She usually got what she wanted, too. She slid into her flip-flops, then pulled her hair back with a band. She sat on the bed frame beside him, then leaned over to give him a chaste kiss.

"You're going to be fine. You did your best, and I'm proud of you. You'll get over the disappointment in a few days." Libby paused, and then said, "I love you, you know."

"Lib," he took her hand and smiled back. "I don't know what I would have done without you last night. I felt so lost. Everything just fell apart. I don't feel much better today, but I want you to know how much I appreciate you being here for me."

Between Libby's attention and the warm, womb-like support of the waterbed, he felt better than he thought he would, though his head still throbbed. The 'L' word had come up a few times, but he hadn't returned it. Not yet. The pressure to respond in kind to her didn't make him feel any more comfortable. He liked her; maybe he loved her. She'd told him she'd wait, but for how long?

"Go see your therapist. She will help you deal with the race. You should take some time off from running, too. You've pushed so hard for so long. It sounds like your body didn't respond and rest might be the best thing."

"Thanks. I'll see Dr. Black later, but I need to run. I'll just do an easy five miles to get the knots out and start the healing. I'll see the good doctor after I run."

"Promise me you'll take it easy? I'll see you tonight." She touched him gently and walked out.

"See you tonight." His smile softened, following her purposeful walk.

****

The two classmates and study group partners in the MBA program became a couple earlier that spring. Libby was self-assured and top of their class in finance and economics. Jeff had caught himself glancing her way more than once in class. She surprised him when she came to ask for running advice one day in the second-floor lounge. She wanted to break 40-minutes in an upcoming 10K race. Sub-40 would make her queen-bee among the women in the local running community.

"Have you ever done more than ten?" Jeff asked, serious about her inquiry and a little off guard giving her advice.

"You're talking about miles not inches, right?" She flashed a toothy grin with just a hint of a blush.

"Yes, miles," he repeated, trying to regain his composure. "A few longer runs will help with the shorter distance. Would you like to do an easy thirteen-miles this weekend." He emphasized miles. Both laughed, sharing her joke and setting the date.

Saturday dawned cold but clear, one of the few decent days that February. Jeff was recovering from a respiratory infection he'd picked up during exams. Semester break had been spent in bed for the most part, so he needed the long, easy run as much as she did. He chose a course that would take them downtown and avoid the big hills, keeping the pace gentle so they could chat, finishing without discomfort.

They ran through the big tobacco warehouses of downtown Winston-Salem. The brick buildings were tall, filled to the roof with the golden leaf. Remnants lined the gutters, perfuming the air with the sweet smell of a pipe store as they passed.

"When did you start running?" Jeff asked. He knew little about her, their conversations in study group normally focused on the case for the next day's class.

"I started in college after doing gymnastics and cheerleading in high school. I wanted to stay fit. I've always been active. I ran some races and got hooked. I get it from my father. We play golf together. Do you play golf?"

"I never have. Golf courses have always been a place to get in a recovery run on soft grass. But I'd like to one day. Looks like fun." There had been opportunities to play with classmates, but the four-hour rounds interfered with his training.

"I'll teach you sometime. We could go to the club. It's only fair since you're helping me with running. I'll probably end up working at my Dad's car dealerships in Charlotte after graduation."

"That's nice that you have a good relationship with your father."

"What about your family?"

"It's complicated. I'm close to my mother, but I find it difficult to measure up to my father's expectations."

"He must be proud of you qualifying for the Trials?"

"He is, in his way. He just doesn't say it. He thinks I'm wasting my time with running. We've had some disagreements over the decisions I've made in my life."

"I think your running is fantastic. You qualified for the Olympic Trials while a full-time MBA student. Most of our class is focused only on the program. You've been able to handle both." Her smile was warm.

They ran in silence. Jeff imagined playing golf with his father. That wasn't going to happen anytime soon. Neither had picked up a club or chased the little white ball, finding their passion in other pursuits.

Jeff and Libby returned to campus, passing the dorm rooms and athletic fields. Libby asked, "So what was your best race?"

"Probably Milwaukee when I qualified for the trials. The last mile was sub-5 and felt so easy. I was in a zone. But the most memorable race would have to be the Lynchburg 10-miler a few years ago. It was just after the Montreal games in '77. A lot of Olympians ran that year for the prize money. I ran really well that day and was trying to recover after a big hill at seven-miles. I glanced up from the pavement and to my surprise, Frank Shorter, my boyhood hero, the gold medalist from Munich is running next to me. He'd just taken silver in Montreal. I could have died and gone to heaven right then. But just in front of him was Bill Rogers, the New York City and Boston Marathon champion. I started to freak out, running with two of the greatest marathoners in the world. I figured I was definitely on the cover of *Runner's World Magazine* that month. "

"Did you get on the cover?"

"No. I think it was Jane Fonda promoting the benefits of Jazzercise that month. But just as I'm getting over racing with Frank and Bill, I look to my right, and there he was, double, double, gold medalist, Lasse-freaking-Viren, the greatest runner of all time. I was in my own Olympic Final. Viren ran like water poured from a pitcher, the smoothest stride I ever saw. I began to hyperventilate, surrounded by that much Olympic Gold."

"Did you win?" She was sincere. Jeff accepted the compliment, distracted by the cute vapor mustache on her upper lip.

"No. Rogers got tired of dogging it and sprinted to the front to win the race. Shorter picked up his pace to finish in the top ten. Lasse and I duked it out the final mile. He out-leaned me at the finish for top twenty."

They finished at Libby's place, where she invited Jeff in for water. He left his shoes at the door and piled his cold weather gear on a chair in the cozy apartment.

"I've got a pot roast and potatoes in the oven. Want to stay for dinner?"

"That sounds great. I don't know the last time I had a home-cooked meal. What time should I be back? I'll get cleaned up and pick up some beer or wine."

Libby walked to him and stood very close. "I thought you could shower here." She surprised him as she shimmied out of her running shorts, letting them fall to the floor. Jeff froze in amazement. With one move, she pulled her tee shirt and running bra over her head, then shook her hair loose. Her tan-lines stood out, her skin radiant from the run. She helped Jeff remove his gear, smiling at his body's reaction to her touch. His damp shirt and shorts fell on top of hers in a pile on the kitchen floor. She led him to the shower, where he touched and kissed her for the first time. Passion overtook the awkwardness of having to wait for the water to warm. The shower was quick, the toweling-off quicker. The two dove into her single bed and each other's arms.

The afternoon ticked away slowly. The two lovers reveled in an endorphin-induced bliss from the run, the sex, and Coors Light sipped between naps in the thin sun that filtered through the blinds. Jeff awakened to Libby's soft snores, curled next to him. Her breaths moved in rhythm to his steady, drum-like heartbeat. A basketball game droned in the background from the small TV; Mugsy and the Demon Deac's were whupping-up on the Tar Heels.

Jeff awoke to a wonderful smell from the kitchen. Libby stood in front of him, wearing his hoodie like a dress that just covered her hips, partially unzipped, her silhouette alluring in the fading light.

"Wake up, sleepy. Dinner is ready, and I'm hungry. Here are your clothes. I washed them but don't get any ideas. That was a one-time deal. Oh, I borrowed your top. Hope you don't mind." She spun and walked out, her bare feet padding on the linoleum.

CHAPTER 3

May 27, 1984, Winston-Salem, North Carolina (later that morning)

Libby's car pulled out of the gravel driveway. The noise brought Jeff back to the present, their tryst the previous February a pleasant memory. She had been a comfort at a low point the previous winter as he struggled to regain his form. It bothered him he couldn't tell her what she found so easy to tell him.

Despite the head-to-toe aches he stretched, needing to move. The waves from the waterbed and uncooperative muscles played against one another, making it difficult to stand. He slipped his legs over the frame, standing gingerly, then pulled on shorts and a tee shirt. Walking upstairs took effort. He poured a cup of coffee from the half full pot in the communal kitchen. Jeff toasted a bagel, checking the cream cheese for green spots before spreading a thick shmear. He chewed his breakfast mechanically, swallowing each bite with a sip of black coffee, feeling energy return. Despite his discomfort, he was eager to get back on the road. He had unfinished business. He needed to run.

Revived, Jeff cleaned up and headed downstairs. The steps down were more painful than going up, his quads and calves locked. Jeff backed down one by one. He pulled on his battered running shoes and a backward ball cap, then slipped on sunglasses as he stepped into the brilliant sunlight outside. Cicadas greeted him with a loud chorus, up in the surrounding oaks.

One of the red-eye bugs came to life in the gravel by his feet and whirred past his head.

"Good morning to you too, boys."

Jeff jogged slowly along the gravel driveway, lurching up the hill to the main road. His toes complained from blisters, his major leg muscles ached, his stride half its normal length. It would take a few days to return to normal. The plan was for five miles through the gardens, an easy run he'd done a hundred times.

The gardens were the beginning and end of most days workouts. They linked the university to the larger community with quaint lanes, a small village of shops and tavern, a large meadow, and forest trails. The gardens were perfect for students playing Frisbee, family picnics, or in Jeff's case, world-class training runs. The estate was a gift to the community from the tobacco baron who's two most popular brands of cigarettes were named after the city.

With each painful step, the previous day's events caroled through his mind. He'd stood on the precipice of his sport and utterly failed. The disappointment from failure hung like a dark cloud, devastating his psyche. He wondered why he subjected himself to the torture. Maybe, he should give up running or take up golf and just be a student? Maybe he should go home and work for his father? Maybe he should try again?

Finishing on the track at the university, Jeff felt nothing but weariness. The bagel and any other stored energy had long since burned off. He stopped, to walk and enjoy the indulgent rest and less pain, soaking in the sunshine. A movement caught his eye.

Across the track, someone waved from the stadium seats. Jeff walked around the curve towards the bleachers, surprised to see old Bill from the Trials.

"Jeffrey," he shouted, his thick white hair brilliant in the sun. He stood slowly, using the handrail to step slowly down.

Jeff shook sweat off his fingers, holding them out apologetically. "Bill, I just saw you in Buffalo yesterday. When did you get to town?"

"I arrived today. I'm happy to see you out and about." Bill might be old, but he certainly had a way of getting around quickly. Aside from the vintage hat, he wore baggy tan slacks and scuffed shoes, carrying his raincoat.

"How did you know that I would be here today? It's a pretty big coincidence I run into you here."

"I come here often for fresh air and to remember the old days. I've often seen you doing your interval work or warm-down. I've become a fan."

Jeff smiled. He tried to recall Bill in the bleachers during workouts on the 400-meter oval. Other than the occasional coed trying to sun herself, the bleachers were usually empty.

"I have fans?" He kicked the rubberized track surface.

"More than you know. I hear the people talk at races. They like your style, taking out the pace and keeping the race honest. You cut a nice profile with your height and the hair, something I certainly could never have gotten away with." He ran a hand through his thick silver locks. Jeff liked his laugh.

"Bill, I don't know much about you. You ran in Amsterdam?"

"Yes. I won the 1928 Trials in Baltimore, my hometown. You should think about running the Baltimore Marathon sometime. It would suit you. You're from Maryland, aren't you?" Jeff pulled against the fence to stretch the big muscles in his legs. It was difficult to think about racing right now.

"I grew up in Maryland, not far from Baltimore."

"There had been two other selection marathons that year. Joey Ray, our fastest man, won the L.A. Trials. The great Clarence DeMar was also on the team. He'd won Bronze at the Paris games in 1924. I had a great day in Baltimore to win the third and final trials race. I think I told you, my winning time and your time at Buffalo were the same."

"Except our outcomes were exactly opposite. You didn't have the meat wagon on your heels. It was so embarrassing to finish last."

"Well, that's our sport, and it's also why I want to talk to you. There is so much more ahead for you and your racing. For me, it's only memories. It was wonderful to win in Baltimore and hear my hometown cheering for me. I still get chills when I think of the day."

"So how did the games go?" Jeff squinted. He wiped his eyes, shaking the drops of sweat from his fingertips.

"I ran poorly. I finished forty-fourth in 2:58. The winner, El Quafi, won in 2 hours and 32 minutes. He was the first African winner, a herdsman, and messenger for the French Army. The medal went to France. It caused quite a disturbance in the Olympic hierarchy with runners from Africa, Chile and Japan taking the top three spots. Joey Ray had a great race to finish fifth."

"The course turned out to be perfect. We ran along the Polder, a bird sanctuary laced with canals and windmills. I fell off the pace from the front pack at 18 and ran in with DeMar and Frick. My day was much like yours in Buffalo."

Jeff listened, wide-eyed and amazed, an Olympian telling him his story and offering to coach him. It was not what he had imagined that morning when he left for his run.

"We lived on the USS Roosevelt while in Amsterdam. I don't think I ever got my land legs back. It was still Prohibition, and the American officials didn't want us hitting the pubs or finding other distractions in Amsterdam. A dinghy rowed us to shore every time we needed to go to the stadium to train or race. But the whole voyage; the team, the outfits, and ceremony, parading in front of the Queen and her Consort, were a once-in-a-lifetime experience for a boy from Baltimore. Buster Crabbe, you know, Buck Rodgers, and Johnny Weissmuller, Tarzan, were swimmers on the team. Both won gold medals. Paavo Nurmi from Finland, perhaps the greatest runner of all time, won his fifth Olympic medal in the 10,000-meters. Our team President was General McArthur. He was a great sportsman and gave each of us a commemorative coin. That coin was almost as good as an Olympic medal."

"We came back home to great fanfare, and my life was never the same. But enough about me, what is your plan?"

"I'm trying to get rid of the pain and loosen up. I feel like I was in a car wreck. I think I want to get back in shape and give the marathon another try this fall. I have to if I want to stay with Converse, my sponsor. I'll have to make the podium."

"Jeff, you don't know me yet, but let me tell you something. I admire your determination and the way you finished the Trials. Now you're getting back up and thinking of the podium. That's the kind of spirit that will take you far. If you want, I'll help you with your next race."

Jeff paused to consider Bill's proposal. "You would coach me? That would be great. I've been on my own since undergraduate school. I could use the help."

"Yes, I would help you. But let's call it advising, you already know what to do. You qualified for the Trials with a 2:18, a fantastic effort. Just take some time to heal and feel better. Easy runs for now, then let's plan your workouts for the fall. If all goes well, we can find a race later on in the year and help you keep your sponsor."

"If you advise me, where do we meet and when? Do you have a phone number I can call?"

"I'm a little unsettled right now, Jeffrey and I don't own a telephone. I never liked the noisy buggers. Let's meet here at the track in the afternoon, after your workouts. If I miss you, we'll figure a way to catch up later in the week. When I get settled, I'll find you."

Jeff jogged off, intrigued by the old man, an Olympian offering to advise him. Jack Bachelor, a more recent Olympian from the Munich games coached some of his Raleigh friends. He had made a difference in their performances. Bill might just be the break Jeff needed. He stopped at the top of the hill to look back but the track was deserted.

CHAPTER 4

Jeff sat opposite Alison Black, a psychiatric resident who worked with students as part of her training. Randy, the head track coach had arranged for her services when things were their most bleak the previous winter.

"Jeff, I'm glad you came in. I haven't seen you since last spring. Tell me how you're doing?"

"Things were going pretty well, but I had a little setback. I ran in the Olympic Trials last week. You might have seen the results in the paper?" He remembered too late she didn't follow sports, preferring the Arts and Entertainment section of the Sunday paper. She shook her head no, making him feel like the slow-witted student called on by the teacher. He continued, a bit red faced. "The race was a complete disaster. I felt I was ready, but then the wheels fell off. I walked across the finished line in last place. Last place for God's sake." He slouched in the chair.

"Why didn't you stop?"

The words stung. "I don't stop and I don't quit. I finish. I've always finished. This race was everything to me. The opportunity only happens every four years, and only the very best get to race. I finally get to the top, and I flop."

"Okay, so you don't quit. Let me ask you, do you like to run?"

"I love running. I'm good at it and always have been. I can do the training required. I've got a sponsor, and I've won some big races."

"I asked do you like to run? Why do you run?"

The question caught him off guard. "When I was in junior high school I wanted to participate in sport. Football, basketball, and baseball weren't for me. It was an eye-hand coordination issue. I was hanging out by the lake after school one day when I saw this fluid white line moving towards me along the water's edge. The cross-country team was out for a training run. They passed me, silent and elegant in their white uniforms. I followed at a distance for about a half mile, winded and out of breath. I became a runner that day and made the team the following year. I'd found my sport."

"Then the '72 Olympic Games from Munich took place. I watched every bit of the competition on TV. Korbut in Gymnastics, Alexia in weightlifting, Sugar Ray in boxing; every sport was memorable. I liked track and field the best, now that I too was a runner. Prefontaine, Wottle, and Viren were gods to me. I'd go out and jog my two miles along the lake after watching the races, pretending to finish with the Olympians. I saw terror for the first time with the Israeli athletes. I had no frame of reference how that kind of cruelty could exist or why they wanted to destroy the games. I didn't understand what loss meant and selfishly, I prayed the games would go on, and they did. On the last day, a Sunday, I sat on the living room floor and watched the most magical and memorable event of the Games. Frank Shorter ran 26-miles through the streets of Munich, largely alone, to win the gold medal in the marathon. I wanted to be a marathon runner like Frank ever since."

"I can feel your passion, Jeff. Have you always run this race, it seems a bit long?"

"No. I ran cross country and track in junior high and high school. I was always second or third best. I'm not the most gifted, but I train hard. I got a scholarship to college where I met my ex-wife. I ran the 5k and 10k in track and set school records before I graduated. Those races weren't long enough for me to make nationals. That's when I took up road racing. I won the North Carolina Marathon Championship after graduation, my first big win. The Olympic Trials was my first National Championship. Failing really hurts."

"I want to get back to the question of why? Why do you like to run so much?"

"When I'm out on the road, I get to see things, things that only I get to see. I like being outside in the fresh air in all the seasons. I think while I run and work things out. I feel good, and my body feels good when I'm running. There's also the reward of finishing. There is nothing like the satisfaction of finishing a long, hard work out and moving through the day with the tinge of the work in my body. The work stays with you and you know there are few who could do what you just did. There is a certain satisfaction in the work."

"Okay, so you like to run. How about racing?"

"Winning is nice, but it's rare. Running well in a race is almost as rewarding as the win. Last year when I qualified at Milwaukee, I felt uncomfortable for twenty miles. But the last six miles were magical and took very little effort. I just let the energy flow. The last mile, my fastest, was perfection. That was a feeling I'll never forget and its own reward. The sports pundits talk about perfection in sports. The perfect dunk or a home run with bases loaded, the athlete who can score at will in an almost unconscious state. The final mile at Milwaukee was like that. I ran at top speed, yet everything went by in slow motion. I could see the faces of the spectators lining the course and the finish line staff. Making the podium is fantastic, and I want to know what that feels like again."

"I'm going to summarize what you just told me. You like to run, and you like to race. You like the things that come along with running: sponsorship, travel, and notoriety. What do you think you'll do next?"

"I'll continue to train. I'll start a new program in a few weeks once I've recovered. I can't quit now, the marathon and I have some unfinished business. I also have a new coach. I think I have the opportunity to break through."

"You sound like you know what you want. Now, let's talk about what happened." She looked down through the wire-framed glasses perched on her nose at the pad, then flipped back a few pages. "You were recovering from a difficult sickness when I saw you last spring. Did the sickness play into your performance at the Trails?"

"I don't know, maybe." He hadn't considered the illness. "That bug knocked me out from December through March. I had a bad cough, and the weather made training outside with any quality difficult. I couldn't get any consistent mileage. I only got my rhythm back in mid-March during spring break. That left a month and a half of good training before the trials. It wasn't nearly enough in hindsight. I hadn't considered the sickness, the lost weight, or lost training days. I guess my body shut down, trying to run a 2:16 race."

"What do you mean, 2:16?"

"My best is 2-hours and 18-minutes. If I ran that time at the trials, I would have been in the top thirty. If I ran 2:16, I would have been top twenty and ranked. It would bring invitations to bigger races and possibly national teams, the big prize in my sport."

"Racing that hard for that long sounds very difficult, yet you love it. Your ambitions aside, what would have happened if you had run easier? Would that have helped?"

"It might have, but the Trials is not a race to run easy. You never know what will happen or how the body will respond over the marathon distance. I probably should have run a more moderate pace."

"Being realistic about your goals is a good start. Disappointment and failure can be difficult to deal with, but that's why we talk. You are disappointed in your race; would you say you are depressed?"

"Depressed? I have no idea. That's your call, Doc. I would say disappointed mostly. I've planned and dreamed of this race since I was a kid. I know everyone says to be proud that I qualified or that I finished, but that's not why I race. Ultimately, it's running well, having a chance, and the overall performance that's rewarding."

"Would a poor performance, like your run at the Trials, make you feel like you did last January?"

"No." Jeff stood. He began pacing, embarrassed by the turn in the discussion. "At least I don't think so. That happened once without a lot of thought. I didn't plan it. I was sick, and tired, and empty."

"Let's go through the events that led to your actions. You went home at the end of the semester."

"I was a sick puppy and lost a lot of weight. I also had a fever, and my cough was bad. My throat felt like it was on fire. My mother nursed me back over Christmas break. Her chicken soup is pretty good."

Dr. Black got up to get a file. "Please continue."

"I recovered, and my throat hurt less after Christmas, but the coughing stayed through March, and my ribs ached. I talked with my father before I left for school. I think that discussion set things off. He didn't want me to become a teacher. He didn't want me to get married. The divorce was just another failure in his eyes. He doesn't understand my desire to race. He wanted me to intern at his company this summer, but I didn't accept."

Dr. Black had returned to her desk. "What will you do this summer?"

"I plan to paint houses for my landlord, the same as last year. It pays the rent, and I make a few bucks for books and food. It's great for training. I have the time to do my workouts, but my father's not pleased."

Jeff focused on a thin crack that ran across the painted cinder block wall. "He had a bottle of scotch in his office. We shared a glass while we talked. That was the best part of the holiday for me, the drink with my dad. There was a fire in the fireplace. It was nice. We hugged goodbye and I didn't want to leave him. I began the seven-hour drive back to school. It was cold and bleak outside, driving back. I thought about him, I thought about Martine, and I became so sad. I took the bottle of scotch with me and drank most it. What I did wasn't predetermined. I can't remember having thought about my actions. I stepped on the gas when I saw the bridge and threw the wheel." Jeff stopped, avoiding her gaze.

"I was lucky. The car missed the bridge column by inches." Jeff paused, breathing a little faster. "I messed this race up, but, no, it wouldn't cause me to," he paused again, "try and end everything." The exact word was hard to say and frightened him. "I don't want to talk about that night."

"I know this is difficult for you, but we need to talk so you can handle your feelings, especially with the outcome of your recent race. We'll leave it for now, but I want you to be conscious of how you feel. We'll come back to this again at a later time. What are your near-term plans?"

"I'm going to recover, train my ass off, and get ready for school."

"Jeff, we just talked about moderation and knowing your limits. 'Training your ass off,' to use your words is a bit extreme. Moderation in training, school, and your personal life is rational behavior. Try to find a balance. Let's stop here today, but I want to continue this talk and make sure you're ready for the fall semester, running, or anything else you choose to do. I would like to see you in two weeks. Check in at the desk on your way out, okay?"

"Yes, I will." Jeff left, happy though exhausted from the discussion. He liked the visits to the doctor, but rehashing the past left him feeling like he'd run twenty quarters around the track at race pace.

****

Jeff returned home to find Matt with the back of his truck open. He was cleaning up after the day, his brushes and rollers soaking and tarps folded. Matt painted houses in the summer and served as Assistant Cross-country coach in the fall.

"So, how's it going? I haven't had a chance to talk to you since you got back. I saw Libby this morning on her way out. I guess things can't be too bad?" Matt winked.

"Just got back from seeing good old Dr. Black. I needed all my ladies help to get me back on my feet. The race was a disaster."

"I read the results. You haven't talked much about it. Finished last, huh?" Matt had competed for the university, an 800-meter specialist back in his day. He knew the disappointment that could come from high expectations.

"Seeing the meat-wagon behind me was more than disappointing. I didn't come back and do all the work last year, just to finish last. I was helpless out there. We also talked about my father. Life just feels crappy sometimes." Matt knew about Jeff's depression, another link in the support team.

"Don't be so hard on yourself. You'll get past the pain. It was one race, and hey, you got to run. Nobody else around here can say that. It was an honor to be there and race to represent your country. And don't be so hard on your old man either. He wants the best for you."

"Yeah, I know. I hope Dad will understand. He wants me up there this summer but I'm going to ramp up the mileage and shoot for something this fall. I found someone to help coach me. His name is Bill Atlee, a former Olympian, and marathoner."

"I'd like to meet him sometime. Maybe we could have him talk to the team this fall? Which Olympics?"

"Amsterdam in 1928. He's pretty old. He will probably be more of an advisor, to help me plan and make sure I don't over-train. We're just work-ing it all out now. I'll bring it up to him and let you know. Since I'm not going home to work for my dad, do have room for me on your paint crew this summer?"

"Sure, I have room. Ride with me tomorrow and get started if you want."

"Great. I'll be ready." Jeff walked into his apartment. He knew he'd be the one to wash out the brushes and fold the tarps the rest of the summer. He didn't mind; painting gave him what he needed; time to run and time to think.

CHAPTER 5

June

Jeff's days were repetitive and dull; run, work, rest, then run again. Recovery eluded him. The physical work of painting outdoors in the North Carolina heat and humidity made him all the more miserable. Normally, the pain and micro injuries inflicted by the race would have passed after a few weeks, but the lethargy and soreness persisted. Training seemed futile.

Jeff ran early to escape the worst of the heat, the morning six-miles a staple. It was always the same run. He'd head across town and come back through the campus gardens. The morning run had one objective; build a foundation. The afternoons were for longer, harder and more specific training. His runs the first two weeks after the trials were all easy, six-miles in the morning followed by an easy three to five- miles in the afternoon. He slept as much as he could between workouts, waking up irritable, tired, and sore.

Jeff stopped to walk halfway through the morning run. His steady six-miles became four. "So this is how it ends, not being able to finish the morning run." He walked slowly, saddened by his condition. Bill waited in the bleachers.

"How was it today, Jeffrey?" His raincoat and hat in his lap.

"Horrible. I couldn't even finish the run. My body hurts. What am I doing? What's the point? My therapist thinks I might be depressed."

"You need a break, and you don't need a therapist. You need to get away to freshen up. Is there somewhere you can go to get some rest? A place to heal, away from work, and school, and running?"

"Libby's family has a cabin in the mountains. We've been there a few times. It's nice and peaceful with wooded trails. I'm sure she could arrange for me to use it."

"That sounds perfect. Take two weeks off, and we'll start fresh when you get back. No running at all while you're away no matter how rested you feel. Walk, hike, and stretch as much as you want, but take the time to gather your strength and refresh your mind. Think about what you want to accomplish so we can focus when you get back. You will need to be 100-percent for the training to come."

****

Jeff stepped onto the slatted porch. The sun shone over the valley below. The cabin perched on a ridge in a hardwood forest at the end of a private, gravel drive. It was his tenth day of solitude on the mountainside. There was no TV and few other cabins nearby. He walked an hour each morning and again in the afternoon on the soft trails, the soreness receding. In between, he read, attempted jigsaw puzzles, and slept. He ate peanut butter sandwiches and frozen pizza for sustenance along with morning coffee and evening beer. Libby would join him later that afternoon, driving up from Charlotte. He was eager for her arrival and conversation outside his head.

The trail descended toward the valley, accompanied by the small stream that babbled noisily beside him. He used the downhill walk to consider the future. He wanted to do well in school this year. He'd used the time at the cabin to catch up on the summer reading list. He also realized he wanted to race again. He knew he could do better.

Bill had given him the schedule he'd follow when he returned. He'd written the workouts in his training journal. When he returned, they'd build up to 100-miles per week, seventeen to twenty-miles each day. There would be some very long training weeks later in July, and August, building his base. Later in the September, he'd add hill training to build strength. October would be faster running at various distances to build top end speed that he could maintain over the distance. He might throw in a few races to judge his fitness. He'd then choose a marathon in November or December. Jeff studied the schedule, anxious to get started.

Jeff stopped at a pool and took off his shoes to stand in the thigh-high, mountain spring water. The hydrotherapy was part of his day, the icy water worked its magic on his warmed muscles, carrying away the metabolic irritants and refreshing the torn muscle cells. He stood in the pool and let his mind wander, following the purple, emerald, and sapphire Damson Flys that skimmed the water. Silver minnows darted around his toes. He rested and recovered.

A shiver from the cool water broke him from his revelry. He put his trainers back on and began the uphill hike back to the cabin. He faced his doubts, could he do it again? Did he have another race in him? Maybe he should focus on school and Libby. The sacrifice had already taken its toll in his life, and he was preparing to do it once again, squeezing in training around his classes and her, running or resting while his classmates studied. He was an anomaly at school but he didn't really care. It dawned on him he liked to train; he liked the solitary miles, pushing his body for five, ten, or twenty miles or finishing off a hard run with sprints on the grass and feeling exhilarated. He'd received a shoe contract and won races regionally, but the big podiums had eluded him. He needed a top finish and fast time at one of the marquee marathons. He'd have to do more, but more was okay. It was the rest of his life, what took place after the finish that troubled him.

Libby. She wanted and deserved more. She wanted to be a couple, fully committed to each other and whatever came after graduation. Managing a relationship and training was complicated, just like graduate school. He felt lucky to have her in his life, and she made a difference, comforting him, being a friend, and softening the hard edges. They were intimate, yet he had not professed his love. How long would she allow that arrangement to continue? He couldn't commit and give her everything and risk failing again. Then there was reality and real life after graduation, another finish line that scared him.

The hike back took his full concentration, stepping over rock and root. He emerged at the trailhead in a full sweat. Libby's car was parked next to his in the paved, stone driveway. Jeff smiled.

****

They sat on the porch swing and gazed into the black night. Lightning bugs flashed intermittently, imitating the heat lightning miles away in the Piedmont. They'd dined on take-out pizza from the one restaurant down in Brevard, and sipped a chilled Chianti she brought for the occasion.

"I'm not leaving. I've decided to become a hermit and just walk the trail and sit in the pool each day like Zonker at Walden Pond."

"Are hermits allowed to have cute girlfriends who visit?" She sat close and ran her fingers through his hair.

"Girlfriends are not allowed. It's in the official hermit manual under things not allowed: good wine, pizza, and cute girlfriends. Tonight's an exception."

"Poor you, then. I'll just have to go back to Winston-Salem and find someone else who wants to have fun. Seriously, how are you feeling after two weeks alone up here?"

"I'm feeling better. I want to train again. It's beautiful, but I'm going nuts with no one to talk to, no newspaper or TV. I've caught up on the reading list for next semester, but I'm ready for human contact."

"Why do you have to run, Jeff? You know it won't change how I feel about you. I love you for you, and you've accomplished so much. Just making the Trials was such an accomplishment. You said it was your goal. Why not call it a career, finish your second year, and see where we end up?"

It would be nice to be normal like every other student in their program. No three-hour weekend runs. No afternoon tempo runs, grinding out mile after mile. No missing parties, vacations, and other parts of life because of the schedule or because he was too tired. He could even take up golf.

"To be honest, I've thought about doing that almost every day while up here. But I've started to miss the training and routine. This week has made me hungry, and I'm not ready to stop yet. I'm good at what I do, and I like the satisfaction from the work. I can't race at this level forever, and that last race will come sooner than I want. I will have to cut back after graduation once I have a career in the real world. To race at this level, and to be sponsored by Converse is special. I want another chance. That's what's been on my mind, walking through the woods each day. I want to race at the top level and have a shot at winning. I want that feeling from Milwaukee."

"What about us?"

Jeff paused. "You know I've been cautious after my divorce. I'm over Martine, but I don't want to risk the same thing happening to us. This time is special, here in graduate school and Winston-Salem. It will change when we graduate."

"I'm okay with change, as long as we're together."

"But this isn't the real world. We live in the artificial environment of the university. I can run because of the schedule and school. It makes our relationship easy. When we leave, work will dictate who we are and what we do together. The pressure and stress of life, real life, can change the dynamics between two people. I'm not afraid to commit to you, but let's go slow. Let me get my training back on track and see how this next semester goes."

"Okay," she snuggled closer. "So what's next?"

"Go back and get my mileage up. I'll run a late fall marathon, most likely Marine Corps in DC. We can make a weekend out of that one."

"No, I mean next. You mentioned you missed human contact." She set her glass down and whispered, "I've missed you these last few weeks."

"You read my mind. I guess running wasn't the only thing I thought of on my walks. I've missed you, too." He kissed her, then took her hand and led her into the cabin.

****

Jeff walked towards Bill at the track. He felt remarkably different, ready for more miles, having just finished the morning six he'd abandoned two weeks earlier.

"So how was the run, lad."

"It was good. Nothing much to report, same old, boring, six-mile run. The difference is I finished. I'm fresh. I know we have to build the base, but I'm looking forward to mixing things up, doing some hills and faster runs for variation."

"Not so fast. You ran into trouble in Buffalo by not building up your base. We're only a month out from the Trials. You've recovered nicely and had a break. I want two good months of solid 100-mile weeks before we add intensity. There is no magic, just miles. Do you hear me?"

"I hear you, and I'm not complaining. It just gets a little boring, doing nothing but base. I've run these roads hundreds of times. Libby went back home, I won't see her until next month, so there's just work and running."

Bill had a funny look. "That's what it takes, lad. No substitute for the mileage. And let me add, you're better off without her here while were building. Women can be a distraction. Take me here or take me there. Don't run today, go with me to the fair. Next thing you know, you've missed your long run for the week. Get your mileage in while she's away before school starts. It will take all your effort, and you can't afford to break down with a fall or winter marathon ahead."

Jeff wasn't sure where Bill was going with this. He didn't like the coach commenting on his personal life. "Did your wife and family ever get in the way?"

"Not in that way. I was always dedicated to my running and winning as a young man. But in the later years, I had to give it up for them, for my family. I was ready by then, but during my prime I let nothing get in the way. We can only run so long before work and obligations take over. So make use of your freedom while you can. Get your mileage up and be in the best shape when the fall rolls around. We'll sharpen you up later on. Then you'll be ready to race."

Bill stopped abruptly to stare at the woods, his thoughts elsewhere, his expression sad. Feeling awkward, Jeff said goodbye."I'll see you later this week, Bill." The old man waved absently.

****

Jeff stood six rungs below the top of the tall ladder, under the eaves of the wood frame home. Today he painted the trim. He climbed down with the paint bucket, moved his tarp, then moved the ladder. He climbed back up with the paint can in tow, hooked it onto the clip and worked as far as he could reach, spreading the light-colored trim around the top boards. He didn't mind, it was breezy and cooler up high, and he didn't have to engage in conversation, preferring to be alone.

Jeff thought about his father. It would have been interesting to work for the man, but his training would suffer. He decided he was better off in Winston-Salem, training and painting.

Libby would be back the following month. It would be nice to have her company, though Bill was right, it did take more effort. Martine had left him due to the grind. Travel to races was no vacation and she had tired of the life of an athlete's wife. Would Libby be any different?

Jeff climbed back down where Matt awaited. "So, how is it up there today?"

"Good. Should be done with the back side by lunchtime."

"I'm taking orders for lunch from Sherwood Barbecue. Let me know what you want, and I'll make a run later. Hey, tonight there's Bluegrass playing in Tobaccoville. Do you want to go? Should be a good night to sit out, listen to some music and drink some brew."

"Thanks for asking. I've got my second workout later and I'm already pretty tired. I'm back to two-a-days, and all this ladder work adds up. I'll let you know but right now I may rest and just watch the ballgame on TV." Jeff gave Matt his lunch order, moved his tarp and climbed back up.

He dipped his brush and began to spread the thick trim paint in long strokes. The painting was similar to running with the time alone and nothing but thoughts. There were a million topics. The painting was also repetitive, like the intervals he ran on the track; paint, move the tarp and ladder, and paint again, circling the house like a tartan track. There was a balance somewhere. He'd had that balance briefly, last summer and fall before Milwaukee. He'd done it once. He could do it again.

CHAPTER 6

July

Jeff ran easily under a periwinkle sky; the persistent soreness of May long gone, his depression shoved back to a quiet corner of his psyche. Running, what he did, was no longer a struggle. Today was the weekly long run, the linchpin of his training week. A good two to three-hour run to start the week and the remainder of the schedule became much easier. By the weekend, his mileage would add up to 120, 130, even 140-miles. The three digits created an efficient stride and well-tuned energy system that allowed him to compete at the highest level. Today's workout called for 19-miles. His track club partners would run 13 with him for company and support. They had obligations he did not; namely church and family. Jeff admired their dedication and pondered the balance, chasing a dream versus real life. One day, he would choose, but not today.

He ran easily, upright and fluid, taking in the lush display, the result of late spring rainstorms and early summer heat. Bright orange Daylilies crowded the roadsides while white and pink Azaleas marched along the borders of verdant green yards. Shade was provided by a gaudy crimson and white Crepe Myrtle canopy.

Jeff glided into the municipal park near the YMCA. He hailed his three friends who stretched lazily in the morning sun. He took several long sips from the fountain, starting off slowly to follow his teammates out of the park. They ran silently at first, eager for the work and time together. The pace was easy, a conversational pace, the warm-up before the real work.

Gradually, their time dropped, mile by mile, just enough to get their heart-rates in range and qualify as real work without becoming anaerobic. The more challenging runs would come later in the week; shorter, faster, and more demanding on his muscles and respiratory system. The four wound up Buena Vista, difficult to distinguish one from the other, shirtless, wearing only light nylon shorts and running shoes. Jeff's friends wore high-end Nike's which they could afford, each gainfully employed. Jeff wore slightly inferior Converse trainers, though his shoes had advantages his friends' didn't; his were free and he had boxes of them at home. The four slipped through the shadows of the tall oak trees along the serpentine street.

"How are the legs today?" Bob inquired. Jeff and Bob were closest among the four. Their friendship had jelled several years before at the Southeastern Marathon Championship in Huntsville, Alabama. The four unknowns from a local club all ran personal bests to beat the larger Nike-sponsored teams. It was a landmark day for Jeff, his first time under 2-hours, 20-minutes, his first national ranking and an indication he could run at the highest level. Converse called soon after with a contract offer; shoes, other gear, and a small stipend to travel.

"My legs feel great for my second week over 100-miles, just the normal weariness in my quads, but good. Nineteen this morning, then five more tonight. I'll finish with twenty-four for the day."

Bob whistled. "Glad it's you and not me. I'll have just started my second Miller Lite while you're still out there getting it done. Aren't you worried about that kind of mileage so soon after the Trials?"

"The time in the mountains did wonders. Besides, I only raced 16-miles at the Trials. I figure I should be able to build on that foundation. If I run high mileage the rest of the summer, I'll have a good shot at a top finish this fall."

"So when you taking another shot at the 'thon?" Ed asked.

"I don't know. We haven't figured that one out yet. Charlotte's too hilly and Huntsville too far. I could run Milwaukee again. It's fast, but I need to make the podium. That rules out New York, too big. Marine Corps is number one right now. It's fairly flat, and I would have a good shot to win. It's only a day's drive so Libby could go with me."

There were side glances and snickers. Ed wolf-whistled. "Okay guys, remember, wives and girlfriends are off limits." Their pace slowed with the laughter.

The miles went by quickly, from the light mood and banter. Running down the narrow state road, they were guided by the tall, bald head of Pilot Mountain on the way out and the downtown bank buildings on the way back. They finished back at the park, slightly faster than they started.

Bob asked, "So who's the new coach?"

"His name's Bill Atlee. He won the 1928 Olympic Trials in Baltimore. Ran the marathon in the Amsterdam Games."

"Wow, an Olympian living in Winston?" Ed exclaimed. "How come I've never heard of him?" The three gathered closely around Jeff, drinking from the fountain.

"I think he's new or just moved here. We met at the Trials, and he offered to help me. I think he can make a difference and help me structure my training. He says he's a fan." No one laughed. Distance runners could be quirky. Guys would run brilliantly one day, then disappear into obscurity the next. Bill certainly fit the mold. "I don't know much about him other than he's from Baltimore. He's pretty old and ran most of his races in the '30's."

"Might be in witness protection or a child molester," Will added with a sinister glance. "I've got friends downtown if you want me to check him out."

Jeff laughed. "No thanks. We'll just see what happens. I'll introduce you guys sometime or see if we can get him to talk to the track club. He has some great stories. I have to get moving. See you all next week."

Jeff high-fived his friends and trotted off, headed back towards campus, navigating the city blocks and manicured suburban yards. When he reached his car, he pulled out a dry T-shirt and draped a towel over his shoulders to save his car seat from the sweat that covered his torso. He took a long drink from the Gatorade stashed in the cooler. A gentle breeze caused goosebumps to run down his arms and legs.

He surveyed the empty practice fields and bleachers, looking for Bill. Jeff shrugged, the fatigue of the run replaced by hunger. He needed to refuel.

One of the compensating factors for the mileage was food. Jeff could eat what he wanted when he wanted. Today was barbecue at the legendary Simoes on the industrial side of town. The old brick building was smoke-stained and sat between two empty warehouses. The darkness inside was disorienting after the bright summer day. The smoldering oak wood, roasted pork, and vinegar bombarded his senses. Jeff put in his order for two chopped sandwiches with slaw, hushpuppies, fries, and a large sweet tea to continue hydrating. He indulged in a frosted mug of Budweiser, a small reward for the days work as he waited. He watched the hefty barbecue boys in white aprons mop and chop the half sides of pork. He picked up his meal in the greasy brown paper and walked to the car. The hush puppies never stood a chance on the short ride home.

****

The reward for the work was a couple of cold beers at Penelope's later that night. Jeff felt accomplished as he entered the bar, twenty-four miles in the log-book, five of those at race pace just an hour before.

The workout was a tempo run at 70 to 80-percent effort. The miles flew by, close to sub 5-minute pace over dirt trails. He ran under a large orange moon that lit the way, finishing at the football fields for sprints. He ran ten, 100-meter strides on the soft grass, jogging just a minuscule amount after each stride. He wrote the word 'invincible' in his diary, his body responding like a well-oiled machine. After a quick shower and two bowls of spaghetti, Jeff joined Matt at a favorite bar for cold brew and conversation.

"Save me a seat." Matt headed to the back of the bar. He'd spotted an old girlfriend, striking up an animated conversation with the woman. Jeff laughed, happy for his friend. He motioned to the bartender for a mug of Stroh's dark.

"Do you mind, lad?" Bill stood just behind Jeff in his big coat. A funny smell had filled the bar.

"Please." Jeff patted the barstool. "You sure get around. How'd you know I would be here?"

"I was finishing dinner when I saw you come in. The Greek dishes remind me of home. We had wonderful Greek food back in Baltimore."

"You want a beer?"

"I would love a National Bohemian. It's my favorite."

"Natty Boh is one of my favorites, too. I threw a bunch of those little brown bottles out my car window in high school." Jeff laughed. "I don't think they have it here. How about a Stroh's Dark?" Bill nodded. Jeff signaled the bartender for a second draught and slid it over to the old man.

"So how did the workouts go today?"

"Great. I put in 19 this morning with my friends. We ran easy, 7:00 to 8:00-minute pace."

"Good. How about the tempo run this evening?"

"It was fantastic. I don't know what it is about running at night. I was flying under that big moon, five-minutes or faster, then striders. I could have done another five."

"Easy, lad. Five is perfect. You're teaching your body to respond at the end of a race when you're tired, switching to a faster pace for the finish. Don't overdo it. There is a balance, and you have to learn to save something for the actual race."

"Okay, I'll hold back. I felt so good." Jeff couldn't decide which he was more excited about, his mileage that day or that he was sitting with an Olympian. He asked. "Tell me about winning the Trials in Baltimore?"

"It was amazing. Baltimore was the final Trials race. There had been two others, one in Los Angeles, and the Boston Marathon. Garvin, a good runner I'd competed against before, took the pace out. I felt great the whole way, and bid my time amongst the leaders. The Millrose boys had come down from New York, so it was competitive. It was also warm, which was an advantage for me. I wore a wetted handkerchief on my head to keep the sun from wilting me. It looked a bit odd, but the trick worked."

Jeff sipped through the foam in his mug.

"I pushed Satyr Hill at eighteen as we came back from the hunt club. No one could stay with me. I took some water from my handler at 20-miles. After that, the win was a formality. They cheered me all the way in, the people, my people, were out in the street. The police cruiser cleared the way. They called me *'Sun Paperboy,'* from my early days with the paper. That's how I trained when I started. My paper route was 10-miles. It took two hours each morning and each afternoon. I would jog the entire route. Largest in the city. The race finished at the town hall in front of hundreds." He paused, remembering.

"Unbelievable. What was your fastest race?"

"2:32 at Baltimore, the Maryland record at that time and my last marathon. I beat DeMar that day and it was hot. I was 30 years old and had to go to work. I would have liked to run sub-2:30, but I concentrated on winning. I won 263 of 284 races in my career. I guess that's enough. I'm satisfied." He paused again.

"That's an incredible percentage. I can't believe I'm having a beer with an Olympian. I met Emile Zatopek once at Frankfurt. He was a real gentleman and one of the greatest of all time. Do you remember him?"

"I do remember him. He ran in the 50's and was invincible then. I was working at Sparrows Point by then and retired but read about his victories in the paper. It was a difficult time for me, no longer racing." Bill stared at his beer in silence but became reanimated quickly. "In my time, the greatest was Paavo Nurmi. I met him in Amsterdam. It's all changed since my day. I don't envy you with the competition today. These African chaps seem born to run."

"Tell me about it. The Kenyans and Ethiopians can go ten deep in the bigger races and I can't do anything about that. All I can do is train as hard and as long as possible, even if I don't win. I'm okay with that outcome."

"There's another way now that we didn't have back then. Some athletes use supplements to recover faster and run longer. You might be able to be one of the best in America and even beat the Africans with supplements. I've seen the effects they have on good athletes that become national and international champions."

"Are you talking about drugs and suggesting I dope?"

"Is that what they call it now, doping? Funny name."

"They've started testing for steroids. I won't do it. I finally got rid of my acne and wouldn't risk that or the other side effects. If I finish top ten or even top twenty but clean, then I'm fine with those results."

"You've just passed your first trial, lad. I wanted to see if you would take the easy route and you didn't. We're going to work fine together. There is no substitute for the road, the hills, and miles. I want you to consider running Baltimore. I know you favor Marine Corps, and the DC race is a good one. But I think you can win Baltimore in December. They would pay your way as one of the invited runners."

"What about Satyr Hill? We always avoided it in school, but my bus drove up every day. It's a monster."

"I won on that hill, and I think you can too. You're a strength runner just like me. Baltimore will suit you well. Just think about it. It's the first weekend in December, so there is plenty of time to prepare, and the weather should still be good." Bill stood and put on his hat. "I'll leave you now. Enjoy your night out. Not too many of those." He pointed at the two beers, his still untouched. "Take two easy days to recover, and we'll do hill repeats on Wednesday. I'll meet with you after that workout." Bill left, followed closely by Matt's friend. A breeze blew into the bar, clearing the musty smell.

Matt sat down where Bill had been sitting. He eyed the mug. "You ordered for me? How thoughtful."

"It was Bill's, but he didn't drink any. You can have it. Did you see him?"

"I wasn't paying attention." Matt still had a big grin. He slurped the beer. "We only looked over once. She wanted to get a look at the famous Olympic Trials runner, Jeff Dillon. Don't let it go to your head. I told her you were just a poor house painter."

"Bill is odd, the way he pops up everywhere. He said he just happened to be eating here. We talked about training, the Olympics, and the Africans. Oh, and we talked about doping."

"He wants you to dope? Don't let Randy hear anything about drugs. He will blow the whistle in a heartbeat. We can't have even a hint of doping around the program with the NCAA."

"Bill said he was testing me. It was just a strange way to go about asking me or finding out what I thought about steroids. I told him no, so I guess I passed the test. Well, here's to old loves and even older coaches, both can drive you nuts."

Jeff clicked Matt's mug and savored the moment; the beer cold, the light jazz, and the reassuring quiver in his muscles from the 24 miles under sun and moon.

CHAPTER 7

Jeff shivered in the hospital classroom that doubled as makeshift office for Dr. Black. The air conditioning hummed on high, a contrast after the heat and humidity of the summer day. He wrote in his diary while he waited. The diary was a constant companion. He transcribed his progress, the good workouts, along with those that challenged him. He also wrote down private confessions to give him insight into good and bad days. He added his mileage for the week.

The doctor walked quickly past and settled into her desk chair. She ran her hand through her short hair, then reached into her bag for pad and pen, pushing her glasses back to gaze at Jeff.

"I'm sorry for making you wait. Rounds went long today."

"It's okay, Alison. Feels like the morgue in here, though."

"I wouldn't say a morgue, but it is chilly." She pulled out a sweater and draped it over her shoulders. "So how are you feeling?"

"Physically I feel great. I'm back up at high mileage. My coach and I have mapped out a program: 100-mile weeks, building toward fall when we'll run some shorter races to sharpen for an early winter marathon."

"One hundred miles of running in a week. That seems excessive?"

"It's what it takes to be able to race twenty-six miles at five minute pace. Sometimes I run up to 30 miles at once. It just depends on the schedule. Hundred mile weeks are bread-and-butter for a marathon runner's training schedule. I'm feeling great. I guess my disappointment from the Trials is fading. The time off helped."

"I'm glad you took time off. How was that? I would be interested to know what you thought about while you were away."

"It was good and I needed the time off. I slept and walked so the muscles in my legs healed. My psyche rested. By the time I came back, I was fired up to train again. It was good to take off and rest."

"I'm glad you did that. Was that your coach's suggestion?"

"Yes, he seems to know me well."

"That's good, Jeff. I think it's great you're training again, as long as your training doesn't become obsessive. We'll talk about your training and racing more next time, to see how you're coming along. Let's talk about relationships today. At your last visit, you mentioned you are seeing someone?"

"Her name is Libby. She's a finance major and one of the top students in the class. I may be passing because of her." Jeff laughed; the doctor didn't respond.

"Is it serious?"

"We are close, intimate." Saying intimate in front of the doctor was difficult. "Libby wants a commitment, and I can't give it to her right now. She said she'd wait."

"Wait for what?"

"I haven't been able to tell her I love her."

"Do you love her?"

"I don't know. We have something nice. Being with Libby is easy. But we're in school, and the real world is completely different. I know from experience." Jeff paused. "I don't want to commit only to have it fall apart once we graduate. She doesn't deserve that, and I don't know if I can handle that kind of failure and personal loss again."

"Let's go back to Martine. I know it's difficult, so take your time. Tell me why you think you failed in your last relationship?"

"I thought we'd covered all of this."

"Let's just review so you're clear what your motivations are with Libby."

"Martine and I are divorced." Jeff paused. "That's about as big a failure as a person can have. She wanted more, and I couldn't give her what she wanted. I may be incapable of giving a woman what she wants."

"And your training. Do you think it played into the divorce?"

"It did. Just about everything is affected because of the time spent in training or recovering. It affects holidays, vacations, weekends. Nothing is exempt. It's a lot for anyone. She got tired of following after me. I'll never forget my last New York City Marathon. We thought it would be a good trip for us to get away. I'd finished and the race took everything out of me. I needed to rest and shut down to recover for a few hours after the race. I crawled in bed. Martine wanted to go out, eat, and have some fun. She'd followed me all day on the subway. We had a big fight, and she left. We worked things out that night, but that was the warning shot. That all took place about a month before she left for good. I never saw it coming."

"So how do you feel about Martine now?"

"That's part of my reluctance with Libby. Martine's leaving still hurts."

"Let's talk about that. Specifically, what hurts?"

"I thought we would always be together. College was ideal when we fell in love. There was no pressure and no responsibility. Then real life and my ambition crushed it."

"How was the last time you saw her. I don't think you ever said how you left things with her?"

Jeff swallowed hard and placed his head in his hands. He didn't make eye contact with Dr. Black as he dredged the memory from a dark place.

"It was at our apartment." He started slowly, staring at the floor. He knew what happened, just not how to say it. "She'd moved out six months earlier. I was packed and ready to leave for graduate school, ready to shut the door on our life together. She came to say goodbye and to pick-up her comforter. It was the only thing I had of hers. That old blanket was a lifesaver all those lonely winter nights." Jeff paused.

"So you said goodbye?"

"I hugged her and was ready to go. We'd never fought and we still cared for one another, though she wasn't with me. She was six months pregnant by then and more lovely than I'd ever seen her. She glowed. We both felt the finality, that our time together was over. I kissed her, but we didn't stop there. We ended up making love, wrapped in the comforter. The vision of us together one last time won't go away, and I don't know if I ever want it to go. There is no way to prepare for the loss, that moment when someone leaves and you understand they won't be back. The loss is unfathomable."

"So how do you feel right now? How does talking about her now, make you feel?"

Jeff looked up and took a deep breath. "There is a writer I like. He covers my sport for Sports Illustrated. An interviewer asked him how he was doing after divorce." Jeff opened his journal to a page near the front. "He said, *"I'm stable, like a patient with a gunshot wound in the abdomen"."* Jeff closed the little book. "That's the pain, an open wound that doesn't heal." He rocked in the chair.

"Are you capable of letting her go? Can you get over the loss?"

"I think so, but I haven't yet. My need to compete took a toll on our marriage. I take full responsibility for what happened, but it doesn't make Martine's leaving any easier. That's the other reason I can't give Libby what she wants. Getting over Martine hasn't been easy."

"What will you do about Libby?"

"I've got to work out my feelings and get over Martine once and for all. I know we're not getting back together. I'm letting go, but it will take time, and I hope the two of us have the time. Then there's the training. I don't want Libby building up the same resentment as Martine."

"Have you asked her? Maybe she wants to be a part of your running and go on this journey with you?"

"That would be great, and she is very accommodating. I don't want her to get hurt. Our relationship has been easy and just fell together. We haven't made any major commitments, but she's told me she loves me. I've held off."

"Just be honest with Libby and yourself. Talk to her about how you feel, even if it is difficult. Figure it out together, and if it works, it works.

If it doesn't work out, then let her know and move on. Let's change the subject. You haven't mentioned your father lately. How is that relationship?

"The relationship is fine, and he's fine." Jeff didn't want to talk about his father, exhausted, and empty from discussing Martine. He wanted to continue with her, to go back to the comforter and pick the scab.

"He came to visit a few weeks ago. We went to dinner at the Village Tavern. He thought it was 'quaint.' We only talked briefly about the trials and my failure. Just one more in a string. We talked about finishing school and going to work after I graduate."

"How did that go?"

"Pretty well. We had a good discussion, and I think Dad might have understood how tough last year was for me. He was happy I was excited about the coming school year. We agree on the importance of graduation. But he was upset I wasn't taking advantage of his offer to work this summer at his firm. He thinks staying here to train and paint houses are both a waste of time. I didn't mention Libby. He never approved of my marriage to Martine and felt our splitting up was an even bigger mistake. I told him I'd be home this winter. I'm hoping he will see me run. Dinner was okay, a little awkward. I find it hard to measure up to his expectations. The man never failed at anything."

"Do you know that he never failed?"

"No."

"Then that is not a realistic expectation. You shouldn't just assume. How much do you two talk?"

"We write, and I call every month. My father doesn't talk much about his past."

"As I said before, keep talking and let your father know how you feel about his expectations for you. Ask him how he handled adversity. You might be surprised. Is there anything else we should discuss, Jeff?"

"I think that's enough for today, don't you? I'm exhausted."

"You have my card and know how to reach me. If I don't hear from you before, I'll see you in two weeks."

Jeff went for a run after the session. It was the only way he knew to process the memories the therapist brought to the surface during their session. He ran south, past the corn stalks, split rail fences, and several fat groundhogs who watched from their burrows. The previous summer, all of his runs were angry. These miles were different, nostalgic and painful. The feelings buffered his exertion. Had it been a year since he had said goodbye to Martine?

Jeff flew down the roadside. The groundhogs scurried out of his path. He saw her, standing in the doorway with just the comforter wrapped around her body. Her long brown hair spilled over her shoulders. But it was her eyes, the green eyes that haunted him.

A horn blared in a long stream. Jeff jumped to a stop, face-to-face with an old, red pick-up truck. He stood in the middle of an intersection. His hands lightly touched the hood.

"Watch where you're going, skinny shit." The truck revved and inched forward.

Jeff backed up to the roadside in a cold sweat. He shook, his breaths rapid. He tried to compose himself. He ducked a beer can as the truck sped off. He looked both ways and jogged on, barely able to put one foot in front of the other. He felt as he had after the trials, devastated and empty. The adrenalin had burned off.

****

The middle of July brought relief from the long miles of training and demons stirred up by therapy. Jeff and Libby attended the wedding of Larry, the proprietor of the local running shoe store and frequent Sunday training partner of Jeff's club group. The affair was small, intimate, and outdoors.

Jeff ordered two Coors Lights from the bar. Pilot Mountain rose up, huge and purple in the dusk. The dark mountain bled into the bright green tobacco that ran up to the field's edge. A bluegrass band played on the porch of the old farmhouse, and the delicious aroma of the pig-picking wafted from the converted oil drum. Libby stood on the edge of the temporary dance floor, strung with lights. The wedding party lounged on the porch, the fragrant smoke of cigars adding to the ambiance.

Jeff placed the beer cans on the small table. Libby pulled him onto the dance floor while a fiddler played a slow, Irish ballad. Her blue gown glistened under the bright bulbs.

Libby placed her head on Jeff's shoulder. "Perfect."

"It is, isn't it? I'm happy for the newlyweds. They picked a nice night." The moon peeked over the mountain.

"We could do this someday," Libby whispered. "It would be just as lovely."

"It would." Jeff paused, anxiety creeping into their dance. After a few moments, he asked, "How can you be so sure?" He looked into her sparkling eyes. "You just amaze me with your confidence. How do you know?"

"I know what I want." She gripped him tighter. "I saw it in class, in our first semester. You were doing something that no one in our class could ever hope to do, training for the Trials on top of an incredibly difficult MBA. But that's not the only thing that attracted me. It's the way you look at people. Do you remember when you went with me to my sister's on the way back from spring break? You met my nephew, Terry. He's got some issues and never allows anyone to touch him. But he walked right to you when you came in the house. He brought you the book about the tractor and sat on your lap to read to him. We all stood there amazed. He'd never done anything like that before."

"I remember. Terry looked like he wanted to play."

"See, that's how I know. You see those who want to be seen, and I want someone like that, like you." Her face was very close. The ballad stopped. The two were alone on the floor, a curiosity to the crowd. Jeff led Libby back to the waiting beers, relieved. The moon was fully overhead. He breathed in the Honeysuckle or Libby's perfume, maybe both. She asked, "What is it like being married? Did you like it?"

Her question surprised him. "I liked it. I liked it a lot. You have this person who is always there, and there's a certain comfort in her presence. Coming home, the anticipation of seeing that face and smile. There is an adaptation, a learning that takes place with each other. Not just the likes, but the dislikes, like underwear or wet towels on the floor. All of that accumulates, and you learn and it's not a bad thing. You grow together and one day find you don't want to be with anyone else." He drained the last sip of his beer. "I need another, how about you?" Libby nodded.

Jeff returned with the beers. He popped both tops. "But that's the good stuff. What they never tell you about is the bad. If someone leaves, the loss of all that shared experience is devastating. Being married while in college was a fantasy. It was too easy. Living in the real world where jobs, and life, and people get in the way is a completely different game. Life is messy. Life is hard. Little things creep in, and one person starts to hold a grudge, or not share anymore, and the dream ends." Jeff stopped. "It's wonderful and difficult, sometimes scary. I'm sorry. I'm a little jaded."

Libby took his hand. "No, that's good, honest. Thanks. Let's go home. I just want to be together." The two disappeared into the gloom.

CHAPTER 8

August

The bell jangled to announce the final lap. The digital clock showed 13-minutes and 31-seconds. Jeff powered over the powder blue track nestled amongst the pines on the Chapel Hill campus. He was enjoying the fluidity of his body, the effortless movement, and shortly, the feeling of the string that would break across his chest.

He drove his arms and lifted his knees into the second-to-last turn. The inside lane was his alone; he'd lapped second place and the rest of the field now ran in lane two. Jeff entered the final straight in full sprint, his long stride eating up the rubber surface. He could see the clock ahead, 14-minutes 31, 32, 33, 34. The clock flashed 35-seconds as he crossed the line. He slowed to a walk. Sweat ran down his body and dripped from his fingertips. The area around the finish line was his for the moment, the other runners crossing the line with another lap to run. He wandered in front of the stands to catch his breath. Jeff waved to the few spectators to acknowledged their applause. Most were family and friends of those still running.

Matt jogged up to congratulate him. "Great run. You made it look easy and lapped the field." The two high-fived.

"Yeah, that's a first, and I highly recommend it." His giddy laughs mixed with gulped oxygen. He could relax now, done for the day. Matt and his teammates were in the final event, the 4x400 meter relay that would follow the 5,000-meters. The relay was the highlight of the championships and conferred bragging rights among the North Carolina Track Clubs.

"You're not done yet. Randy wants you on the relay. Danny couldn't get off work. He needs you to run the third leg."

"Are you serious?" Jeff expressed mock displeasure, happy to be part of the relay. What's one more lap? A full sprint for 400-meters wasn't that much different than the lap he'd just completed.

"Yeah, serious. Go get your spikes on." Matt loped off to prepare. Jeff walked to the bleachers to change out of his comfortable racing flats for his spikes. The shoes were lighter, custom fit, with small metal grips on the toes. Jeff laced each shoe and walked gently to the area where the relay teams assembled, conscious of the mild fatigue.

Randy, the university's head coach, approached Jeff. He slapped the Old-Gold and Black striped baton into Jeff's outstretched hand. Fit and energetic for a man in his 50's, he'd won the gold medal a few years before at US Senior Nationals in the 800-meters. Like all the other competitors on the track that day, Randy wanted to taste victory one more time.

"Think you can break 70-seconds, sport?" Matt, and Tim, the other two members laughed. "We'll do the heavy lifting. You just need to stay reasonably close and hang onto the baton. I'll close the deal." He gave Jeff a knowing look and patted his shoulder. "Godiva is the competition. All their guys are former sprinters, not marathoners." Jeff joined in the banter, happy to be included. The humor eased the tension of the moment. The prospect of sprinting one full lap at sixty seconds or less and one-hundred percent anaerobic was a bit daunting.

"Considering I just broke seventy seconds after twelve-laps, I'd say yeah, I'm ready. Appreciate the vote of confidence, Coach." Jeff had asked Randy to coach him the year before. Randy had declined due to his obligations to the university. He'd also confessed that his knowledge was limited to the track and not the road. He'd graciously extended the invitation for Jeff to run with the team whenever it fit his schedule in compensation to show the undergrads there was athletics after college.

The starter called the teams to the line. Matt led off, their second fastest man. He performed a series of jumps in his lane to blow off steam, white paint visible on the back of his tan calves. Jeff looked down to see if his legs were similarly speckled. The second runners backed off the line to stand in the passing zone, ready to receive the baton. Rick would run second. Jeff had the third spot, reserved for the slowest of the four. Randy, the fastest, would run anchor. The two waited off to the side.

The gun sounded. Matt tucked in behind the taller Godiva runner, heavily muscled, he most likely specialized in the 100-meter and 200-meter sprints in college. Now, like most of those racing, he'd traded in his spikes for a button-down shirt and tie at one of the Research Triangle firms. The club race gave the thirty and forty-something runners the opportunity to remember what it was like to be fast and fearless, if a few pounds heavier.

The two raced down the back straight. Matt worked hard to keep up with the pure speed of the larger man. A 10-meter gap opened between the two with the rest of the field strung out behind. Entering the final turn, Matt picked up a few yards as other runner began to tire. Matt handed to Tim, who closed the gap in the first few strides, dead even with his man. Jeff walked to the line. He took a few bouncy steps as Matt had, his spikes making pock-pock noises. He stood in the second lane and took a deep breath, prepared to take the hand-off.

Jeff danced a little jig in the acceleration zone, preparing. He'd have only twenty-meters to receive the baton without disqualification once he started his sprint. He watched Tim approach at full speed, contorted in his effort. He took a couple of dainty steps, hand out, judging Tim's approach, the calm before the chaos. Jeff felt the aluminum baton slap into his palm and launched into a full sprint, a half a stride behind Godiva's third man. He attached himself to the runner, the tall man's heels grazing Jeff's thigh. The two raced around the curve and down the backstretch, inches apart. He was breathing hard, his arms and legs moving in unison.

Jeff could feel the final sprint. It loomed just ahead, calling him. He knew he was fitter than everyone who raced that day though not as fast in a flat out sprint. He was also fully warmed up after the 5k. The power welled within, energy dammed, stored and harnessed for the right moment. He waited, motoring down the backstretch in a lower gear. When he reached the curve, he let the energy flow. It poured from his body, legs churning, arms clawing the air. His spikes barely touched the rubber surface of the track. Jeff pulled away from Godiva's man to hand the baton to Randy with half a straightaway lead. The 50-meter advantage was a gift Randy used to full advantage. They won by a full 100-meters.

The four rode back to Winston-Salem in Randy's old Plymouth, buoyed by the win. Two gold medallions hung from the colorful ribbons around Jeff's neck. The club championship trophy sat between Jeff and Matt in the threadbare back seat, buried in McDonald's Filet-O-Fish and French-fry wrappers.

"Matt said he got your split in 59.9 seconds, Sport." Randy's eyes were mirthful in the rearview mirror. Sub-sixty was a big deal to a guy who's normal pace was in the 70-second range.

"Yeah, I'm happy. That's my first 400 meters under a minute. I feel pretty good considering the heavy training." He sipped a tall Coca-Cola.

"You know there will be an asterisk next to your P.R. since you had a running start," Matt added. The others found this hilarious; they'd all run in the mid-50's.

"That's fine, guys. You speed merchants can have your one and two lap races. If any of you want to run a man's race, you can join me for 12 or 24-laps. Oh, I forgot," he jangled his medals, "did anyone in this car earn more than one of these today?"

They returned to the university as night fell. The four said their good-byes. Jeff stepped gingerly from the car, alarmed at the pain in his ankle. He felt a little knot in his right Achilles tendon, painful to the touch.

Jeff heard someone approach. He turned to see Bill, surprised by the old man in the dim parking lot light.

"How did it go? It looked like you have a bit of a limp?"

"I ran a great race today, but I might have overdone it. I ran unchallenged in the 5K in 14:35. The club needed me on the relay, so I wore my spikes. My Achilles tendon is a little tender. I ran a 59-second 400-meters dash." He expected Bill to be impressed.

Bill turned away slowly and gripped the metal fence that enclosed the parking lot. His body shook and the chain-link fence rattled. Jeff caught a whiff of something foul, a rotting, burnt odor.

Bill turned back to Jeff, eyes wide. "I told you nothing fast, boy," Bill snarled. "What were you thinking of letting them talk you into running a sprint? In spikes, no less?" He was close to Jeff's face, his breathing rapid. The smell that came from the man nauseated Jeff. His McDonald's dinner roiled in his stomach.

Jeff took a step backward. Pain shot up his leg like electric current. He gripped the car door and grimaced. "Bill, hold on. Don't get so upset. The race was my choice, with my friends. I laced those spikes. A little ice and rest and it will be fine." He stood straight and shot back. "Let me remind you we don't have this," he leaned towards Bill, despite the odor, and gestured from one to the other. "We don't have the kind of relationship where you make demands on me. You are here to help guide me and nothing more. You don't get to tell me about my choices on the track, the road, or anywhere else. I'm not going to feel threatened and what is that smell? Did you crap your pants?" He stood his ground, prepared to leave.

"No, I didn't crap my pants and don't say such things. I don't know what you are talking about." He continued, "You can't afford a slip-up like this, Jeff. There is too much at stake. You have one chance this fall." Bill's shoulders slumped. He stuck his hands in his pockets and took a few steps back. The stench had passed.

"I'm sorry I got angry. Running still means something to me. You're right; we don't have the kind of relationship where I can tell you what to do. I hope you'll forgive me?" Bill stared at Jeff.

"I forgive you, but stay out of my face." Jeff relaxed his grip on the car window, still blocked from leaving.

"Take it easy for a few days with gentle stretching to heal. Let's check in on Saturday and see if you're up for an easy five. I've got a special workout I want you to try soon, and you will need to be 100-percent. That workout will prepare you for Satyr Hill and give you the ability to finish a marathon strong, but the injury will have to heal fully. That's why I got so angry. I want you to do well this winter, and I can see the progress. You ran 14:35 with no rest and no speedwork off of pure mileage, plus the 400-meter sprint. You're strong and fast, and this shows we're on the right track."

Jeff decided not to engage the old coach about Baltimore and Satyr-fucking-Hill. "Okay, Bill. I'll take it easy. But, you take it easy too." Bill backed away and Jeff pulled out. He left the old man slumped against the fence.

The conflict bothered Jeff. The smell as they argued bothered him too. Was it old man smell, a combination of must and mildew, from clothes too old and unwashed? Did he have an accident or a colostomy bag? Something could have blown over from the tobacco plant, ammonia perhaps. He'd been so eager for the Olympians help that he hadn't checked the man out. What if Will was right and he was psycho or worse? Jeff made a mental note to find out more about Bill. He could use the computer lab at school once the semester started. The new, inter-college library system might turn something up. He shook off the dust-up, happy to pull into his driveway.

Jeff walked gingerly upstairs for ice from the refrigerator and slouched on the couch in the communal living room. Matt had on the Summer Olympic games from LA. Jeff propped his sore heel on an ice pack and opened a Heineken.

"Hope you don't mind?" Jeff tilted the beer at Matt who also sipped one.

"No problem. What happened to you?" Matt kept a supply of the green bottled beer in the refrigerator and never tired of telling anyone who asked that he needed more greens in his diet.

"I don't know what happened. I got out of Randy's car, and my tendon was inflamed. Hurts like hell and my coach had an absolute fit."

"Your coach, Bill? I didn't see him when we dropped you off."

"Yeah, he showed up out of nowhere and got in my face. He told me I was foolish to wear spikes and sprint a four-hundred. It was kind of strange. He apologized, so I guess we're okay." Jeff let the dust-up with his coach go, turning back to the LA games. The cold beer and ice were the perfect tonic.

The Twenty-third Olympiad became an afterthought after the Trials. In the past, the world class competition would have fueled Jeff's training like nothing else, running for miles while fantasizing about the racers and races. Jeff ignored most of the TV coverage and caught up on the results in the morning paper over coffee. Maybe it was the over-the-top Hollywood treatment that caused his dismay. There was one bright spot with the inaugural women's marathon. The race was another miracle in the history of the iconic race. Joan Benoit of the US and a former runner in the Carolina's with Jeff left the world behind on the hot asphalt streets of LA for a lonely run to gold.

The U.S. men had the opposite experience, falling victim to heat and injuries, their performances anticlimactic. Jeff suspected the poor showing might be due to the crucible that had been the U.S. Trials, the US runners leaving their best racing on the parkway between Buffalo, NY and Canada. The games concluded and Jeff clicked off the TV. The siren that was his waterbed called and there were miles to be run the next day.

CHAPTER 9

The large Tudor home in the Arts District needed paint, primarily on the exterior where it had blistered and peeled over the years. Matt's crew also were painting the inside, touching up where it was needed. Jeff worked alone indoors on the upstairs trim, while the rest of the crew were staining the exterior. This would be his last job before the new semester.

Jeff entered the large, master suite. His footsteps resounded on the polished floors of the empty house. The room was stuffy and claustrophobic. With some difficulty, he slid open two windows, their sashes rough and over-painted. Despite being open, there was no breeze. He spread his tarp and opened the trim can to pour the cream-colored paint into the tray, then climbed the ladder. He dipped his brush and began to spread the paint on the crown molding in long steady strokes.

Jeff immediately felt drowsy from the warmth and smell of oil-based paint. Skynard serenaded from outside on Matt's boom-box. A wasp buzzed against a window across the room while cicadas droned. One of the windows slammed shut, startling him. He climbed down and raised it again, using a paint stirrer as a prop to keep it open. As he turned to climb back up, the opposite window slammed shut. He jumped, deciding to leave it shut.

Jeff worked his way around the room. In the back corner near the shut window, he noticed a rancid smell. He fanned his brush like a nosegay to dispel the odor, strong one minute and gone the next.

Finished with the crown molding, he folded the ladder and started on the chair rail. Halfway around the room, he heard footsteps approach the room from down the hall. No one came through the open door. Jeff peeked into the empty hall. He went back to his work, moving around the room. Once again, soft steps came down the hall. The footsteps stopped outside the door. Jeff put down his brush to step into the hall. The guys must be fooling with him. The door slammed shut behind him, causing the hair on his neck to prickle.

Jeff reached for the knob, unsure if he wanted to reenter. The knob turned and he opened the door. He stepped inside to an empty room and the heat of the summer day. The wasp still buzzed. He walked across the room and picked up his brush, returning to the rail.

Something touched his shoulder. Jeff jumped. "Oh my God."

Matt stood behind him, amused. "I didn't want to scare you. It looks like I failed." He laughed.

"You scared the crap out of me. Geeze."

"Sorry, it's lunchtime. How about Bell Brothers?"

The thought of lunch helped him forget the spooky old room. Jeff sat up front in Matt's pick-up, the rest of the crew in the truck bed. Matt told Jeff about the old woman who had died in the master suite of the house he painted.

"A neighbor found her after several weeks. She'd died in bed. The air conditioning had been shut off. They found her badly decomposed, a neighbor was alerted by the smell."

"The smell is still there and I swear I heard footsteps. Kind of creepy in that room."

"Jesus, I leave you alone for a few hours, and you go bat-shit-crazy on me. You think there's a ghost?" Jeff didn't know what he thought. His only experience with the supernatural had been in books, TV, or movies.

"I don't know what I think about ghosts. But, I do hope they have ham or fried chicken on special at Bell Brothers. Pair that with green beans, mac-and-cheese, a sweet potato biscuit and sweet tea ought to do the trick." Jeff would need those calories to fuel his afternoon training session.

****

Jeff returned to Dr. Black, anxious to talk about the coming semester. She came out to the seating area and motioned him into her office.

"Hello, Jeff." He rose slower than normal, walking in.. "Are you limping?"

"I have a little tendinitis in my Achilles. I ran a low-key track meet and overdid it. I'm not too worried. Ice and aspirin work wonders. My coach or advisor or whatever he is, flipped out when he found out about my injury. We had a big shouting match after the meet." She didn't say anything, so he continued. "I also painted a spooky house. Do you believe in ghosts?"

"No, I don't. I can only help you with the figurative kind, the people and events from your past that haunt you." Jeff nodded. "Why do you ask?"

"I was in an old house where a lady died recently, but I didn't find that out until later. I felt a presence and I heard noises that I can't explain. Twice I heard someone walking down the hall, but when I looked, no one was there. There was also this really bad odor. It shook me."

"It's normal to be spooked by the unexplained. If you have other experiences you can't explain, please tell me. Otherwise, I don't think we need to talk further about the house and footsteps. You are sensitive and perceptive and that's not a bad thing. I wouldn't worry about it further." She smiled.

"Now," she continued. "We talked about loss several weeks back. Have you had any new revelations about Martine and what happened between you two?"

"The pain from the divorce is still there. I don't dwell on it. Last year I was so angry, and that pain was always on the surface. Training hard and your therapy helped. Now its a year later I don't think about the loss much. The pain is minimal. I've read how people who lost limbs still feel an itch from a foot or hand that isn't there any longer. I've learned not to notice."

"You're unhappy?"

"No, not at all. I have good friends. I have a great living arrangement. My training makes me happy. Libby is such a comfort and my best friend. She's been wonderful. My family is good, and school should go well this year. All these things are wonderful and I value them. There is just that slight ache or pain there from the past. Sometimes I wake up at night, and there is this deeper loss. It passes by morning."

"Good, Jeff. We're going to keep working on the pain. It will go away. Let's talk about school since it starts soon. Are you feeling any pressure?"

"A little, but I think I'm ready. It was close. I almost didn't come back." Jeff wiped his forehead in mock relief.

"Why is that?"

"The school is selective. If the grades and first-year project aren't up to standard, they let you go. We lost ten from the first year and I was right on the cusp. My grades were okay. I passed even though finance and accounting kicked my butt. Libby helped. It was the first year project that almost sunk me."

"How so?"

"My partner and I did our marketing project at a local hospital. It was a feasibility study for a satellite office at a neighboring hospital. The results were overwhelmingly positive, so we decided to skip the marketing analytics. We would have had to retype our paper with the new results for the added charts and graphs. Libby was begging me to go on spring break with her to Florida. I was recovering from that illness over the holidays. My preparation for the Trials had suffered due to the heavy winter. I was a mess last spring if you remember. The prospect of sun and sand was too hard to resist. So we turned in the paper and I headed south with Libby."

"So what happened?"

"The defense of our paper didn't go so well. The three professors who were to grade us walked in and I was so nervous that I dropped the slides for the overhead projector. When I stood up, I wasn't in a position to shake hands. I raised my hand and said, "Hey." Jeff held his hand up flat in a casual wave.

"Professor Mason, the biggest curmudgeon on the faculty, said, "'I will not 'talk to the hand as you students like to say, Mr. Dillon. Gentlemen shake hands.'" Then he started a rant I'll never forget. He said, "'Let me just say that this is by far the worst project in my tenure at the university. If it were up to me, both of you would fail and removed from the program. I will not waste my time with you here today.'"

"He left the room and I freaked out. I looked at my partner, then asked the other two professors if we could continue? I think they felt embarrassed by their colleague's behavior. They asked us to proceed, and we rallied. We passed with two B's and an F. I scooted into the second year by the seat of my pants." Jeff shook his head in wonder.

"Would you say, to use a business phrase that the risk was worth the reward?"

"You could say that." Jeff answered, recalling the week down at the Gulf. "The trip to Florida did wonders for my health and training. Going to Florida made life worth living again. I would train each morning while Libby slept. I ran tempos on the state road between the mile markers and hill work on the causeway. The warm gulf air was great for my cough. I felt my strength return. We ran together in the afternoons on the beach and ate fried shrimp or oysters each night. We picked oranges and grapefruit from the tree in the courtyard each day. I came back rested and ready for the second semester and the Olympic Trials. It was a fantastic week."

"Okay, so how do you think this year will go?"

"Good. I have the confidence to handle the subject matter with a year under my belt. The fact that I made it back means I belong. I know how to study, and the hard courses are over for the most part. I'm even taking Mason's marketing course. I went to see him and he encouraged me to take it. He said he had no hard feelings. I think I'll graduate next spring."

"Where does your confidence come from?"

"Lots of things, it's an accumulation I guess. There was one moment last fall when I felt like I belonged. I had just returned from Milwaukee and my qualifier. No one in the class knew me that well or what I was trying to do. They knew I ran a lot, but everyone was so focused on the program. The only person who knew my ambition was my project partner, Vince.

"I walked into our classroom the Monday following the race. Vince had written on the board, '"Ask Jeff what he did this weekend.'" The sports page was open with the article highlighted on our desk."

"Dr. Luther came in to begin economics and asked, "'So Mr. Dillon, tell us what you did this weekend?'"

"We sit in an auditorium that holds 60 students. I stood and told the class I had qualified for the U.S. Olympic Trials. They all stood as one and gave me a standing ovation that went on-and-on. Classmates slapped my back or shook my hand. Other professors came in to see what was going on. It was amazing and a feeling I'll never forget."

"It sounds like you are ready for the year to begin. Is there anything else?"

"There's only this weird dream I keep having. My normal dream is presenting to class in my underwear or going to a race and not being able to make it through the crowd to the starting line. I know those are just anxiety. This one is different and strange. It started after the Trials, and I didn't give it much thought. It's probably a childhood memory. But lately I've had it almost every night. I'm in an old car from the '50s. My parents had one like this, pea green vinyl seats and body paint. The music from the radio is the kind my parents liked, Sinatra I think. It's dusk, and the car has been parked in a seaside area with old buildings around it. I can see a big stone church and boats. A crow caws from the street lamp and flies off. The car is running, and there's a rubber hose in my hand."

"Is that something you've thought about?"

"You mean sitting in a running car and sucking carbon monoxide from a pipe? No. The memory may be something from childhood, like I said, when I was sitting in a running car. I'm not going to try to hurt myself again. I don't know where this is, and everything seems old. I've been waking up exhausted."

"The dream bothers me, and I think we need to talk about it more. If it continues or if graduate school gets to be too much, I want you to call. Let's take a break today and check back in two weeks unless you feel the need to see me sooner."

Jeff walked out, relieved to share the dream that had become part of his early morning wake-up. He'd completed the therapy on his psyche and now needed therapy on his tendon.

****

Jeff ran toward Hanging Rock, the lonely mountain his destination. The state park's sister, Pilot Mountain, stood to the west with its tall, bald head. He felt revived after an easy week, maintaining a steady tempo. His tendon felt better, stiff that morning but now loose and pain-free. His watch said he had been at it for an hour and one-half. He ran rhythmically, easily. He expended little energy, looking forward to the change of scenery and the climb. He'd leave the flat corn fields for the shaded woods of the mountain. He'd entered the park and ran past the check-in station toward the first switchback. He had a 1.5-mile climb to the 2,500-foot summit where Libby waited. She had dropped him off for the twenty-mile run, then drove ahead with the cooler to sun herself on the exposed rocks.

He ran mechanically, as the climb began up the mountain road. The switchback elbows provided a quick respite with each climb, working his way up the mountain, his quads firing, creating a slight burn. On one switchback he had to jump over a very long, surprised black snake that also sought the sun, more concerned for his tendinitis than the snake. Jeff walked a few steps, checking on his gimpy Achilles tendon before resuming the run. A short while later, he entered the upper parking lot and slowed to a luxurious walk. His Celica GT was just ahead in the parking lot. He walked the narrow, brushy path to the overlook.

Libby lay on a towel, her tangerine bikini contrasted with the gray stone and blue sky. Jeff stood behind her, careful not to drip on her back.

"Nice view," he said, taking in the girl, the rock, and the valley floor below.

"Are you talking about the valley or something else." Her voice was sleepy.

"Oh, just everything."

"How was your run?" Libby rolled over and sat with a hand to her eyes from the sun.

"Great. The climb wasn't too difficult and my Achilles felt fine. Glad it's starting to feel better." Jeff took off his shoes, the rock cool on his feet.

He reached into the cooler to pull out a Gatorade. A few drops of the ice water splashed on the stone and soft green moss.

"The view is incredible from up here." Jeff walked to the lip and stood, the valley spread before him. His toes gripped the rock ledge.

"I know. I love coming up here, though it would have been nice to be on the Yadkin River today, tubing with the rest of our class. I thought it was a nice way to kick off the second year."

Jeff put the Gatorade back in the cooler and took out a beer. He sat next to Libby and stuck his heel in the ice. "You know I can't take off from training right now. This run was critical after the time off to rest my tendon."

"It's one day. You couldn't take off one day."

"I told you to go without me."

"Who would pick you up and drive you home from here? You seem so inflexible sometimes. I think a day in the river would have been great for your tendon."

"It would. But I'd miss the mileage and with school starting, I'll miss some workouts because of class. Look, I'm not always going to run or have the time to train. We graduate next spring and we'll both have jobs. This year may be my last at this level."

She didn't respond, paging through a magazine.

"Did I tell you about the house we finished painting this week?" It was a good time to change subjects.

"No, but I noticed your work." She pointed to his legs and the white splatters.

"I'm happy that may be the last house I ever paint." He laughed to lighten the mood. "But that wasn't what I wanted to tell you." He relayed the story of the slamming doors, the smell, and the footsteps. Libby didn't flinch. "Do you think there are ghosts," he asked.

"I've never seen one, but yeah, I believe some ghosts or spirits stay on earth for whatever reason. There is this old Civil War cemetery near my home. It's a private family plot in the middle of a farm field. I love to go there and sit. I read the gravestones or read books. Sometimes I feel someone or something there, a presence. I've never actually seen anything but I think there is more than we can see."

"So I'm not bat-shit-crazy like Matt said."

"No, you're not. You're just goofy." She opened a Coors Light.

"Are you ready for class to start?"

"Yeah. I'm ready to graduate and get on with life, whatever that brings."

The unspoken future hung above them like the hawks that circled above. "Libby," he began. "You made life bearable for me this year, and I can never repay you for that. I was in a very bad place most of last year and almost didn't come back after Christmas holiday." She started to speak, but he hushed her. "Let me finish. It was an accumulation of things. It was my past, and school, and home."

"And Martine."

"Yeah, Martine." He hadn't said her name much in front of Libby. It felt good to say her name out loud and let some of the air out of that unspoken part of his past. "I thought about not coming back to school in January, not coming back at all." Jeff had not shared the failed suicide with her. "I was in this very dark place, and then you came into my life. I found reasons to go forward, and you were a big part of that. I'm excited about graduation, too. I just want you to know what you mean to me. Let's get this semester under our belts and see what comes our way." She accepted his proposal with a smile. They clinked beer cans like champagne glasses.

"If we leave now, we can meet the class at the landing spot down at the river. I think they're going to barbecue. Want to go?"

"That sounds good. My bony ass is sore from these rocks. The water will feel nice."

Jeff surveyed the valley below. "You know with school and training, we'll be busy and there won't be many more days like this."

"I'm not worried. We'll find the time." They walked up the path, arms around each other.

"Did I tell you about the snake I saw." Libby gasped and grabbed Jeff tighter. "Oh, not here. It was down the road a bit."

"Bastard."

CHAPTER 10

September

Jeff took the steps two at a time in anticipation of his first class. He took his normal seat, back row-left, eager for the class and school year to begin. Vince, his first-year project partner, dutifully studied the sports page.

"Hey, Vince," Jeff held up his hand.

"Gentlemen shake hands, Mr. Dillon." Jeff laughed as they high-fived.

"I still can't believe our project passed. Did I tell you I signed up for Mason's marketing course this semester? He said no hard feelings. I'm looking forward to learning from the old bastard. His knowledge of marketing and advertising is legendary."

"I'm going to pass on that one. I got enough of Mason in those thirty seconds when he blasted our project."

"That's 30 seconds neither of us will ever get back. How was your summer?"

"I worked a lot, ran a little. Twenty to thirty miles a week. I'm in decent shape. I'd like to run the 8k in October. Are you going to run? You're defending champion."

"I have to check with my coach. I'd like to. I've been at high mileage all summer so I could use a break. I've got a December marathon in Baltimore."

Dr. Mel walked into the room. The tall man stood at the lectern and moved his glasses down from his large bald head to study the class. "Welcome, to Organizational Behavior, second-year students. It's good to see everyone and I trust you each had a fulfilling summer. Who would like to summarize the case regarding the Clancy Street Gang?"

Jeff raised his hand.

"Mr. Dillon, please proceed."

"The Clancy Street Gang is more of a social group than a gang as we think of them in modern times. The cities on the east coast had large immigrant populations in the nineteen-thirties. Due to the depression, there was little work. The immigrants often formed groups or gangs for security, social reasons, and to pass the time. The gang boss ruled with his lieutenants, those members he could trust. The boss and the hierarchy often carried over to the manual labor jobs that were available. The newest members had the lowest rank for errands and unskilled jobs that needed to be carried out. It could be difficult for the man who lived in that neighborhood or workplace, and was on the outside, shunned by the inner workings of the gang."

"Eventually, the unions took over the workplace, providing worker safety, fraternalism, and benefits, the same things the gang had once provided. The evolution of the gang to today's modern workplace is still observable. In a school, there is the principal and vice principal and their teachers, who operate in a similar hierarchy, a bit less formal. Another example could be a bank with the branch manager, loan officer, and tellers. Instead of a street corner or bowling alley, the group passes information at the water cooler or on the golf course." Jeff sat, satisfied with his summary.

"Thank you, Mr. Dillon. Very concise. Now let's take a little deeper dive and review the economics and social dynamics of the gang in this time-period."

The class filed out ninety minutes later relieved, the first class of the semester complete. Dr. Mel stopped Jeff.

"Mr. Dillon, I was happy to see you raise your hand this morning. Your summary was well done. Where did you find your insight?"

"I'm excited to be back and I found this case interesting. I have a friend who advises me on my running. He's from this era and worked in the steel mill at Sparrows Point in Baltimore. I've heard his stories of the gangs at the mill back in the early forties and fifties. He doesn't make it sound like it was all good times and fun at the bowling alley."

"The thirties and forties could be tough times. I'd like to interview your friend sometime if that's okay with you? His stories would be a wonderful addition to this case study. Maybe we could have him speak to the class?"

"I'll ask him. He doesn't go out in public much. He's turned down offers to talk to the track club, so I'm not sure."

"Very well. Just let me know." The two parted, and Jeff headed for the Pitt, the campus grill, needing to refuel before the afternoon run. He quickly fell into the old routine: morning run, breakfast, followed by class, then eat a quick lunch, attend the afternoon session and take a quick nap before the second workout. He would then refuel on leftovers from whatever was cooked Sunday night or stop by the K&W cafeteria before study group. The evening finished with notes from the day or reading of cases before a well earned sleep.

Bill walked in and sat in the vacant seat across from Jeff. His clothes were rumpled and hair uncombed.

"I didn't expect to see you until later in the week. Are you feeling okay? You look a little rough."

"I'm okay, Jeffrey. I've had a few tough days."

"I'm sorry you're not feeling well."

"I'm just feeling my age. I've had little energy. It takes a lot for me to get out and about."

"We can cut back our meetings to once a week if you want. I know what to do in the workouts. Would that make things easier for you?" There was the slightest scent of the foul smell that often entered with Bill. Halitosis, Jeff decided.

"Thank you, that's kind of you to offer. No, I'll be fine. I need to be here and when we work together, I feel better. I'll get my energy back. You seem full of it. Are you ready for the capstone run? That's the reason I came to see you today."

"I'm ready, though I'm a little nervous, we've planned for this all summer. I get out of class early tomorrow and thought I'd do it then. I'll have plenty of time and quite frankly, I'm ready to hit the gas a little."

"Good. I want you to run hard but no more than sixty percent. Warm-up well and pace yourself. If you have a bad patch, try to work through it. If you feel good at the end, I want you to hold back. No extra miles. Better to quit with fuel in the tank and recover than to wear yourself down and risk injury. Proper training is about getting in the work over the training cycle. It's the culmination and build-up of all those miles, not just one good workout. That's the key and why you had such a hard time at your Trials. You didn't have the build-up or consistency like you've had this summer."

"I see all of that in hindsight. I wish you'd shown up last spring. Hey, Bill, do you think I can race soon? There is an 8k next month. It's a local race that I've won a couple of times."

"That should fit in well with what we're doing. Let's see how you handle this workout and then we can make plans to race. We'll do the capstone again, later this month and twice in October. We can use the race as a tempo run in between."

"Great. The defending champion will be on the starting line." Jeff held his arms up signifying the win.

"I always liked the local races." Bill reminisced. "My last one was the church festival race at my parish. It was a small, five-mile race into the city with the finish at the church carnival. We raced in the evening and I won by a large margin. They carried me off to the grandstand for the trophy. I remember it like it was yesterday."

"I like festivals, too. The Camel City race kicks off the festival that celebrates the city's tobacco heritage. It's always fun to finish and have a few brews with the track club, listen to music, and enjoy the food."

Bill closed his eyes, resting. He opened them with a start. "Sorry. I'm a little tired. It's time for my afternoon nap. If you don't mind, I'll take my leave. Let's talk after the capstone." Bill stood, stiffly.

"Rest up, Bill. I'll see you later this week."

****

Jeff headed north from campus on the capstone run. The first few miles he ran easy, warming up. He had to admit he was excited about the day's work, his muscles lose and ready to work. The pace dropped steadily from 8, to 7, to 6-minute mile pace. Nearing the fifth mile, he turned onto the state road that headed back toward town and the first hill. He raced to the top just shy of full speed, noting his arm and leg action. Jeff relaxed on the downward side to prepare for the next uphill and steady his breathing. He began to recover, then raced up the second hill, this one slightly longer and a bit more steep. The cycle continued over the next five miles; sprint the hill, ease over the top and recover as best he could before the next repetition. His body accumulated the by-products of spent energy, lactic acid, the tell-tale sign from the burning in his carotid arteries. His legs ached with each repetition. The last hill was the longest, a full mile in length with a steep grade near the top. Jeff reached the summit exhilarated, taking tiny steps and breathing as much oxygen as he could take in. He wanted more but held back the impulse to double back. Instead, he ran toward campus for the third and final section of the workout on the grass practice field. Without stopping, Jeff jogged to the starting line for the makeshift four–hundred meter grass oval. He cleared his watch and clicked his timer to circled the field, driving his arms and legs over the soft grass. He hit the timer as he crossed the 300-meter mark. A short hundred-meter jog followed, then he sprinted again; straight away, curve, then straight before the jog to the faded chalk line. Jeff clicked the watch for the eighth and final time. He ran eight, 300-meter strides to simulate the final two miles of the race. His reward for the work was a luxurious, slow mile on the soft grass. He removed his shoes to feel the short blades tickle and massage the bottom of his feet. The football team trudged out to practice while he stretched, lazy and happy to be finished as they were starting. Sixteen quality miles, twenty-two in all for the day with energy left in the tank. He walked to the locker room, content in the knowledge he had finished a workout that a very small number of people on the planet could complete.

****

Jeff dodged bikes, a wagon, and boxes of chalk on the sidewalk that led to the crowded porch. He knocked on his friend's door. Catie, Bob's wife, greeted him. She handed Jeff a cold Coors's Light and a gave him a peck on the cheek.

"The old man's out back. Dinner will be ready in 20-minutes. Bob said you took it easy on him today."

"It was the other way around. He took it easy on me. I needed him to pull me through today after the capstone run yesterday. I was more tired than I thought I would be." Catie scooted off, the kids and kitchen called for her attention. Jeff popped the top of the can, slurping the first sip. He headed out the back door.

"Bobby." His training partner sat in a lounge chair beside a table with a stack of magazines.

"Glad you could join us for dinner."

"You think I'm going to miss Catie's cooking? I love coming here and being a part of your happy little family." Bob's golden retriever joined them, slapping her tail against Jeff's legs. Jeff scratched the dog's head.

Bob picked up one of the magazines. "I needed to show you something. Are you still working with that coach? What's his name?"

"Bill Atlee. He ran in the 1928 games."

"Did you ever check him out?"

"I've been meaning to but haven't had the chance to go to the library. Why do you ask?"

"I remembered something. Atlee's name rang a bell and I wanted to make sure it was the same guy. That's why I asked you. It took a while to go through my old *Runners World* magazines. Remember this issue from a couple of years ago? You were in the results for the Cherry Blossom Classic."

"I remember."

Bob opened the magazine to a page with a paper clip. He handed it to Jeff. The article announced the Road Racing Hall of Fame inductees. Near the bottom, Jeff read five words that Bob had circled in pen. *William Atlee, Baltimore, Maryland, Deceased.*

80

He pulled the magazine closer, *William 'Bill' Atlee was a 1928 U.S. Olympic Trials Men's Marathon winner. He placed 44th in the 1928 Olympics in Amsterdam with a time of 2:58.50. He died in 1953.* The picture showed a much younger Bill, with thick black hair and wide grin as he broke the tape held by a fat man in a top-hat on the old streets of Baltimore.

"Is that your guy?"

"That's his name. And the photo looks like him though he's much younger in the picture. I don't know who my guy is. This conversation and that magazine article do not make any sense."

"What are you going to do?"

"I have no idea."

Catie came out, "If you two are finished discussing heroes and ghosts, then dinner is ready."

The two filed into the house. Despite the wonderful smell coming from the kitchen table, Jeff's appetite had disappeared.

"There has to be a logical explanation. Do you think we should get with Will and have the boys downtown check him out?" Bob asked.

"No, let's leave Will out of this for now. In fact, can we keep this among the three of us? I probably need to talk to Bill or whoever he is, and find out what's going on."

After dinner, Bob and Jeff cleared the dishes, then washed and placed them on the drying rack. "What are you going to do?" Bob asked.

"I don't know. Confront the old devil, I guess. We meet in plain sight, so, I'm not scared. I don't see how this could happen? Why would someone take another person's identity? Another question is why I'm involved? It's not like I'm ranked number one or make a fortune on the road race circuit? We're talking about the Camel City 8k and Baltimore Marathon for God's sake."

"Don't know what to tell you, buddy. Be safe. If you want me to be there when you talk to him, I will."

"I should be fine and thanks but Matt's usually around after practice so I can grab him if I need back-up. He's eighty-something years old, so I don't think I need to start doing push-ups. I better get going. Thanks again for dinner and for showing me this. I'll call you after I talk to him. See you on Sunday for the long run."

Catie walked him to the door. "Be careful, Jeff. Bob and I talked about your coach. Sometimes, the real world is not as it seems. There are a lot of kooks out there and other things we can't explain and you're a nice guy. You're probably too nice. Stay in the sunlight." He hugged her goodbye. Her new age wisdom cheered him until he stepped into the dark street where his car was parked.

****

Jeff snuggled with Libby, unable to sleep. He hadn't confided in her about the troubling article. He needed a plan, constructing a decision tree and assigning probabilities to potential outcomes. It amused him that business school statistics had a practical side. On the one hand, Bill had been a big help; his workouts were going well and a good winter race seemed likely. But Bill as an impostor troubled him. He couldn't assign a probability or an outcome to that reality. Only Bill could provide answers. If Bill was not who or what he claimed to be, Jeff would terminate their relationship. He'd made his decision.

He slept in fitful spurts that night, troubled by the same disruptive dream he had since returning from the trials. He sat in the old sedan with the engine running while the radio played softly. He coughed over and over while the engine rumbled.

When he woke the next morning, he felt anxious and unrested. He needed answers and ended his training run on the track, hoping to find Bill. His anxiety grew as days passed with no sign of the man. The secret wore on him, and he found it hard to focus in class.

Jeff left the gym after practice at the end of the week. A familiar figure sat in the bleachers across the track. He walked around to him, nervous but determined, the evening sky darkening. Bill had on his raincoat, as usual. He removed his big hat as Jeff arrived.

"Bill, we need to talk." Jeff walked up the steps to stand in front of him.

"What's on your mind? Is it the capstone workout? Tell me how you thought it went?"

"I wish it was about the capstone. You're supposed to be my coach. Are you my coach?" Jeff paused and took a deep breath. "You never told me you were inducted into the Road Racing Hall of Fame two years ago. That must have been quite an honor."

Bill's brown eyes were clear and piercing and his hair well groomed, different from the disheveled old man in the campus cafe. Jeff caught a whiff of the strong odor, the same smell from the confrontation after the track meet.

"I did get into the Hall of Fame but wasn't able to attend the ceremony. I couldn't attend, it wasn't possible. It was nice to be recognized but none of it means anything to me now." He went silent. Jeff wondered what would come next. "I'm going to tell you a story. Please let me finish before you make up your mind or try to leave."

CHAPTER II

"I loved running. I was good and I won, I won a lot. I liked the notoriety, the hardware, and I got to travel. I was able to see the states and the world. I was in the *Baltimore Sun* sports section almost every weekend in the late '20s to the mid-30s. Everyone knew me, especially after the Olympics. But I never made any money. The Depression was hard for my family and me. I never went off to college and I missed the two wars. I was too young for the first and too old for the second. Eventually, I had to leave the paper and find regular work. I was married to Charlene by then, and she was pregnant."

"I took work at Sparrows Point, the big steel mill in the Harbor. They were hiring and the wages were good. I took the bus like all the other fellows down to the mill. But it was hell. The place was always dark and either blazing hot or bone-chilling cold. It was dirty, grimy work. I never saw the sun. My knees and ankles began to ache. The bosses and men could be brutal. They didn't like having a man who had been somebody on their shift. I never expected to be in that position, having a family that needed me and a job I hated, a job that destroyed me, day-by-day."

"That doesn't answer my question. Who are you and why are you coaching me?" Jeff held up the article in the fading light. A light turned on in the track office above them.

"I'm going to tell you something. You may not believe it at first, but I want a promise." Jeff started to protest, but Bill continued. "I want you to promise me that no matter what I say or what you think after I finish that you won't change your mind about the race. I understand it's a lot to ask of you, but you must run the Baltimore Marathon."

"It would be kind of hard to change now. I talked to the race director this week. He's sent me the tickets, hotel voucher, and waved my entry. My manager will be there, and my family is expecting me. Yeah, I'm up for Baltimore."

"Promise me, Jeff."

Jeff didn't give it much thought. He could always bail out and switch the tickets or pick an earlier race. "Sure Bill, I promise." He sat on a bleacher seat.

Bill paced the narrow walkway past Jeff. The rancid-burnt smell wafted by with the flowing coat, making him slightly nauseous. Jeff breathed through his mouth.

"The Point wore me down day after day. I couldn't face the work, the conditions, the men or their taunting anymore. Life became unbearable. I drank too much and didn't always go home. I met someone and it was difficult living two lives." He slowed and stopped with his back to Jeff. "One day, I just had enough between the men at work, my priest, my wife, and the other woman. It was too much. I walked out of the bar and drove my car behind the church. I left the windows up while the car ran and I went to sleep for a very long time."

There was no breeze, but Jeff felt chilled. Goosebumps ran down his arms and legs. Bill had described Jeff's dream, the one he'd had since the Trials. Jeff wrapped his arms around his knees for warmth. He listened, wary of the man and his story.

"I was proud of my work that day." He chuckled. "Funny that the last thing I ever did turned out so well. I left the car running in neutral with the parking brake on. I took a length of plastic hose from the trunk, fit it into the tailpipe and sealed it with tape. I fit the hose through a piece of cardboard cut to fit the back window and taped it all in place, nice and snug. I opened the driver's door and climbed in. The radio station played the night-time hits. I thought about Charlene and the boys as the radio played. We used to listen to that station when we went for ice cream. But I was more tired than sad at that moment. I was so tired that it hurt and all I wanted was to sleep. You know how that feels, don't you, Jeffrey?"

Jeff didn't answer, but he did know that hollow, tired feeling. Tired of the arguments, of the anxiety, tired of life. He had been that tired once. He listened in disbelief, unsure of what to do.

"I went to sleep. I slept for a long time, and now I'm here with you." Bill stood facing the track with his hands in his pockets.

"You committed suicide," Jeff blurted. His next words surprised him. "You're a ghost?"

"Yes, I live in the spirit world."

"How does this work? I don't understand? Am I going insane? Have I imagined you and all this? Maybe this discussion is another one of my dreams. I think I need to leave. I feel sick."

"Stay." Bill's voice was strong. Jeff stood, ready to run.

"Please stay." Bill turned to face him. "You can't leave. It doesn't work that way. You can walk away, but I leave with you." The statement sunk in with cold reality. Jeff wanted an answer, but not this one. He needed to get away no matter what Bill said.

Jeff started to walk past Bill, but he grasped his arm. His grip was strong, the touch cold, and the smell unbearable as the stench enveloped him. "Please, let me finish."

Jeff breathed rapidly. Adrenalin pumped through his veins, and his heart thumped in his eardrums. Bill released Jeff's arm, throbbing where his fingers had been.

"You can go whenever you like. I'm not holding you here. But you and I are linked. The dream you've had is about me and my suicide. You asked how it works and I don't know the whole answer. For so long I was nowhere and nothing. For years I slept. Then I was around Baltimore, the old pub. Then I was gone and one day I found myself at a road race. I enjoyed being out with the boys in the sunshine and fresh air. I attended many races which were so much nicer than the nothingness. I realized after a while that you were at each of those races. I've followed you the last few years as you developed into a national competitor. I realized you were the reason I was at the races, the common link. I saw everything that happened to you during that time, the good and the bad. I witnessed the break-up of your marriage and the despair that followed. You were deader than I was when your marriage ended. I thought you might end up like me and we'd be two spirits passing time together. I was on the highway that night when you tried to end your life."

"You were you there?" Jeff asked softly. It was incredible how he knew about Martine and the drive home from the holidays. There was no one on the road that night but Jeff, and a crow in the headlights. "The Crow. Was that you Bill? Are you an angel?"

"Not quite." Bill chuckled. "No, I'm no angel. It's pain that links us and draws us together. That's why you can see me and others can't. I need your help though I don't know what that is yet. I think it's obvious that you need my help. I couldn't let you go out the way I did." Neither said a word. The two sat in silence, a man and the form of a man. Jeff's thoughts spun. Nausea in his gut grounded him back to reality, talking to a ghost in the bleachers. The light went off in the office.

"How do I help you? I don't understand?"

"I don't understand it all either. I know we're bound together. I need to get home. I think you're here to help me do that." Both were silent, then Bill spoke, "I know what I've told you is difficult to understand. Take some time and think but don't dwell on the situation. It is what it is, and something beyond you or me has linked us. I promise I won't burden you."

"You mean you won't haunt me."

"I won't burden you but you need to keep our arrangement. Honor your word and I'll stay away. We can meet here after workouts. Let's plan to meet next week after your long run on Sunday. Go to class, run and rest. I'll see you next week. Congratulations on finishing the capstone run so strongly. I saw you finish. You're coming along fine."

Bill walked down to the track. He took several steps then smiled at Jeff before he dissolved, a faint trace of foulness noticeable. Jeff rocked in his seat, his head in his hands. "This can't be happening," he told himself.

****

Jeff and Libby sat in the booth of a local Japanese Steakhouse they both liked. He picked the restaurant to have the conversation about Bill, needing to share what was happening. He needed to confide his secret, only slightly relieved to know the truth. Jeff wolfed down his plate of grilled steak, rice, and vegetables, ravenous from his training but also nervous about telling Libby about his haunting. He helped Libby finish her plate, sipping a tall, Sapporo beer or Japanese Budweiser as he liked to call it. The first went down quickly. He forced himself to sip the second, getting his courage up. A large, rice paper wall hanging caught his attention. It featured a crow perched on a pine bough above rushing water. The bird's eye was the size of a golf ball, bright orange, with a piercing black pupil.

"You seem distracted. Not just today, but this whole week. Is something wrong?" Libby probed.

"You could say that. Something is very wrong. I don't know where to begin."

Her posture shifted. She sat up and set down her wine glass. "Convenient we're out in public. That's where these things usually happen. I can't make a scene here. It's Martine, isn't it?" She turned away, her arms crossed.

"I wish it were that simple. I don't mean that the way it sounds but a conversation about our relationship would be easier if you can believe it. What I have to tell you is not about you and me or Martine, although what I have to say affects us both. I'm happy you're here with me and that I can confide in you. I need you to get through this, and you're going to need another glass of wine."

"Okay, you have my attention and you're scaring me. What is it?"

Jeff signaled the waiter for a second glass of wine. He took a deep breath and pulled out the magazine article. He handed it to Libby.

"What does this mean?" She scanned the sheet.

"Bob gave that article to me. That's my coach." Jeff pointed to the high-lighted text. "He died in 1954." He stopped to let the disclosure settle. "I confronted him, and he confirmed the article is correct. He killed himself and that wacky dream I've been having is how he did it. He described my dream exactly as I've seen it even though I've never mentioned it to him."

Libby held the copy of the article up to read closely. "What does this mean? Is this a joke, because it's not funny."

"It's not a joke. Bill's a ghost and he's haunting me. He says we're linked. When we met the other day, he disappeared into the night and has this strange, otherworldly smell. If I've seemed distant it's because I'm having a hard time believing I'm haunted and he's a ghost."

"You believe him?"

"I don't know what I believe. You told me you believe in spirits."

"I do, but they don't meet me at the track after practice. When did you see your therapist last? I think you need to talk to her about this. You might be seeing things. Maybe school and training are too much. I'm serious, Jeff." The waiter delivered her drink. "This discussion and that freaking crow on the wall are giving me the creeps."

"I've felt the same way all week, the creepiness. I don't know what to do. I don't want to tell Dr. Black yet. She's going to think I'm completely nuts and have me committed. I don't want to have to leave school or interrupt my training when I'm so close to a breakthrough. I'll understand if you think I've lost my mind. You won't hurt my feelings if you have to walk away. Just keep this between us. It could get messy if our class or professors found out."

"I'm not going to leave you over this and I'm glad you confided in me. I do believe in more than what's visible, but this is preposterous. What are you going to do?"

"He asked me to keep things the same. He won't haunt me, sorry, link to me outside the track if I keep our arrangement and go to Baltimore."

"Let's say for argument's sake that I believe you. Can Bill see you and see us anytime he wants to?"

"He can see everything I do and he's been hanging around me for the last few years. He only decided to get up-close-and-personal after the Trials."

"Ew," she drew the sound out in disgust. "Now I'm freaking out. Can he see us in bed? Has he been watching us for the last eight months? I'm sorry, I'm dressing under the covers from now on and I don't want to do it anymore if he can see us."

"I think he's more interested in me than you. He considers you a distraction."

"That's even creepier. Ghost or not, do you realize he's threatened you? Do what he says, or he will keep haunting you?"

"I don't see a choice. I think Bill needs to get back to Baltimore and somehow, I'm involved. It had to do with my breakdown last winter before you and I got together. The connection has to do with the pain Bill and I both faced."

"Do I need to worry about being a distraction?"

"I don't think so. We agreed up front that Bill has no say in my life outside of running. It's simple. I need to finish my training cycle, fly to Baltimore and race. He needs to get home, but I don't know what happens after that."

"But what happens if you get there and it doesn't end?"

"I don't know, but he's adamant about our agreement. I guess I can hold him to the same agreement."

"He's a freaking ghost, Jeff. You can't hold him to anything."

"Don't get upset, Lib. I don't have enough information yet. I've got to let this play out. Bill and I are talking later this week, and I'm going to ask more questions. I'm also going to go to the library and read up on spirits to see what my options are. If it gets too weird and you need to get out, I'll understand. But I'm glad you're here. I needed to tell someone."

"Promise me you'll go see your therapist. I want to make sure you are all right. Just when I thought our second year was going to be a walk in the park, my boyfriend starts seeing ghosts." She placed her head in her hands. Jeff placed his hands on hers, his head gently touching hers.

"Now you know how I feel. There aren't any answers that make sense. I didn't ask for this. I'm sorry you're caught up in my haunting."

Jeff paid the bill and walked out with Libby. She insisted they drive to her apartment and Jeff stay. He performed a check around the apartment at her request, then watched in amusement as she closed the curtains tight and undressed under the covers. Libby slipped on a flannel nightgown despite the warm night.

CHAPTER 12

The only respite from the haunting and questions with no answers came from training. Jeff happily joined the team for weekly hill repeats. It helped to be with friends, his fears set aside for the time being.

Randy blew the whistle for boys to form a small circle and gave them the workout. They would run Buena Vista's 800-meter hill six times, averaging 2-minutes, 40-seconds per interval; hard but not all out. Jeff would pace the group to ensure they hit the times Randy wanted. Matt jogged off to the top to catch their split times.

Jeff moved to the front at the whistle. Rob ran at his side with George, the two blue chippers on the team. Whitey, Layne, Stevie, Darryl, 800 and 1,500-meter specialists strung-out behind. Matt clicked the watch in 2:42. The first interval came off as planned, the group finishing in a bunch. Darryl pushed the second interval, the speedy miler racing ahead. Jeff let him go, unwilling to sacrifice the workout for one repetition. The talented junior paid the price for his exuberance. He lagged behind as the group jogged back to the start and sat out the third repeat, hunched over as he regained normal breathing. Randy called off the shorter distance guys after number four. That left Jeff, George, and Rob to finish the six under Matt's watch. They ran the last two in the low 2:30's, faster than the previous four but within themselves, the familiar burn in the lungs and legs from the burnt fuel that accumulated in their bloodstream. The two undergrads led the way back to the locker room, happily chattering about the season as they recovered. The topic switched to Jeff's upcoming marathon and road racing, the younger guys hungry for information and what it was like to race on the road. They soon settled on music as the conversation often did, punk versus classic rock, the Clash versus the Eagles. The youngsters were adamant about their position and Johnny Rotten's legacy. Jeff and Matt shrugged with indifference, the warm-down chatter enjoyable, the icing on the cake savored after the hard work.

"When are we going to meet your coach?" Matt asked.

"We've decided on advisor rather than a coach. I asked him about speaking to the team, and he's not interested right now. He's older and gets tired easily. I'll ask him again once my race is out of the way. We're pretty focused on that one." Matt seemed satisfied with the answer.

Coming through the gardens, Jeff saw Dr. Bailey, his accounting professor out for his afternoon run. Jeff said goodbye to the cross-country boys and peeled off. Bailey ran slow, the tortoise from the fable. Jeff enjoyed their infrequent jogs together when they would discuss school, life, and travel. Jeff felt it was no coincidence that he had passed first year accounting by the narrowest of margins due to their friendship.

"Dr. Bailey."

"Jeff, I don't want to slow you down. You and the boys were moving right along."

"That's okay; I wanted your advice about something."

"Go on." The two jogged back up the hill Jeff had just run down.

"You've traveled a lot and you've mentioned Vietnam. Have you ever had any experience with the supernatural?"

"I don't know. It depends on what you call the supernatural. I hook up my airstream and travel every summer. I've seen most of North America and some of South America and Mexico. I've been out alone on the prairie and desert and seen and heard things that I certainly could not explain. Is that what you mean?"

"What do you know about ghosts or spirits?"

"Not much and I haven't given the topic much thought. Is something bothering you?

"Maybe. I don't know enough yet. I had an experience with what I think is a ghost. I don't know if I believe in such things. But since I saw it, felt it, and smelled its presence, it has to be real, doesn't it?"

"That's all outside my field of expertise. I saw things in Nam that would turn your stomach and make your hair stand up. Sometimes, I didn't know if those things were supernatural or human. Let me give you some advice just in case things get too strange."

"What's that?"

"When in doubt, run like hell."

Jeff laughed, thinking of the tall, thin, CPA in camo, loping through the jungle in Vietnam.

Bill waited in the stands as Jeff and Dr. Baily finished their run. Jeff said goodbye to his professor and walked over to the far side of the track. He was on full alert and waved half-heartedly in Bill's direction. Jeff stood on the track, unsure of the conversation since the circumstances surrounding their relationship had changed so drastically at their last meeting.

"Good work, lad. Looked like you and the college boys put in some good repetitions on the hill."

"Bill, I don't think I can do this. I'm having a hard time processing our relationship. Libby's concerned and I'm worried that I might be hallucinating. Maybe I need to see my doctor. She can probably fix all this with medication."

"You don't want to tell her. She will close the door on you and you won't come back the same person. You've seen what happens to people who see things."

Jeff was amazed once again by what Bill knew. "You mean, Harriett. My student the year I taught." Bill nodded. "She went from being a state champion in cross country to an in-patient at the hospital on heavy medication. She was Schizophrenic and never completed the tenth grade. It was very sad."

"Stay away from the doctor. She can't help you. You'll only be unhappy by what she tells you if you confide in her. You are not seeing things and medication can't help you. If you tell her, she won't let you run the race in

December. You should also let go of this other little girl you're seeing. She's not going to stay with you with the stories you're telling her. You should cut your losses. Just run and study. It's enough."

Jeff didn't have the energy to fight Bill.

"Why did you do it? Why did you take your life?"

"I wasn't well and I hurt. Not just physically but in my mind. My family had needs I couldn't provide. I'd never failed and then all of a sudden, I couldn't win. I came to a very dark place where I couldn't face the stress of life. Just like you."

"I made a spur-of-the-moment decision." Jeff added quickly. "I didn't plan it and I'm glad it didn't happen. I'm happy to be alive and have a second chance. I've found there's so much to live for even when I'm unhappy. I've learned to live with the losses in my life."

"There is a lot for you to live for but first things first. I want you to keep your distractions to a minimum. Your school is enough. This young woman you see, you need to let her go."

Jeff gathered his courage. "What is it about you and women?"

"I was married and met another woman. There were demands put on me that I couldn't address and it ruined me. Don't get me wrong, I loved my wife and the boys. But I couldn't give them and the other what they wanted and needed. I could have kept running and winning if it wasn't for my responsibility to my family. I don't want you having the same issues, getting involved and having to cut back. Everything's going so well. You are close to your best."

"I've said this before, Bill. Libby is not part of our bargain. It's you and me, got it? I make the decisions outside of running and you have no say. You want to haunt me, that's fine, but leave her alone. I'm going to need all my friends if I have to deal with you in my life."

Bill backed off, his hands up. "Whatever you want. You decide. I'm just saying a relationship can wear you down. Her needs, a woman's needs, can be excessive when you are training like you are right now."

Jeff decided it was time to leave. "I've got to go, Bill. When I met you, you presented yourself as an advisor. Now I find out you're a ghost. I didn't bargain for this when we decided to run Baltimore. Our arrangement, as you call it, is about you and me, and I'm willing to go forward for now so that you can go home and leave me alone. But Libby stays out of this no matter what. Quite frankly, this whole discussion is pissing me off." Jeff took a deep breath to calm himself. "What comes next?"

"We keep working. You need to race, and we're going to add some faster runs."

"I need to go. This relationship is exhausting and all I want to do is sleep. I'll see you later this week." Bill faded from view with those last words, a silvery shadow in the moonlight. Jeff shivered. He walked slowly to his car, in doubt about everything that had taken place in the last few days on the cozy campus.

****

Jeff paced across Dr. Black's office despite Bill's admonishment. He was not sure what he'd say.

"What's bothering you, Jeff? Is it your classes?"

"My classes are fine. My running is fine. My relationships are fine."

"Then what's causing the anxiety?"

"I can't tell you yet."

"Why can't you tell me?"

"Because you wouldn't believe me and I need answers first."

"How am I supposed to help if you can't tell me?"

He thought for a few moments. "There is one thing I can tell you. It's about my coach-advisor. I should have checked Bill out better. He is very controlling, and I'm having a hard time with his demands."

"Is it the workouts?"

"No, the workouts are great. It looks like I'm going to be ready for my winter marathon. I'm at a level I've rarely been at and I don't see that changing. Bill's asking me to drop Libby. I told him to mind his own business. My personal life has nothing to do with him and what we are trying to accomplish."

"Does he know of Martine and your struggles with personal relationships in the past?"

"Yes, he does."

"Maybe he's concerned for you. He might be worried that you'll get hurt again."

"It's none of his business. We have an agreement that he advises me on my running and nothing else. I made it clear."

"Is there anything physical or threatening about the relationship? Did he do anything that has you worried or may have hurt you?"

"No, he hasn't threatened me. He's eighty-something, so I'm not worried physically. But there is a lot of psychological stress. Bill insists that I race in Baltimore and that we have an agreement. He won't coach me after that."

"Why Baltimore? Why is that location important? Aren't there other races like New York and Boston?"

"He won Baltimore long ago and thinks I can win it, too."

"What aren't you telling me? You've told me about a disagreement between two people and I don't hear any violence or malevolence from what you've said to me. If you are upset with him then maybe you need to separate. If he continues to bother you then report him to campus security. You don't have to run in Baltimore. Why don't you consider running somewhere else?" She paused, considering her next words carefully. "I want you to consider dropping out of this race. I don't think it's a good idea that you travel right now and put so much pressure on yourself to perform before exams. I'm going to consult with my supervisor. I think it might be a good idea to get him involved and get a second opinion. It was this time last year that you first came to see me after the attempted suicide. We can prescribe medication for your anxiety. It will make you feel better as you approach exams."

"I've got to watch the medications, Doc. They are starting to test at the bigger races. Can you check and see if any of those medications are on the Olympic Committee's banned list? I'll let you know if anything out-of-the-ordinary happens. We can schedule a consult with your supervisor after the race and before exams if you want but I am going to run. I can't waste the shape I'm in. I need to make that podium."

Jeff left her office feeling better for unloading his burden even though he'd only disclosed half the situation. At least he could tell Libby he'd met with the doctor. There still were questions. Was he hallucinating? Did he need medication or hospitalization? Maybe he'd lost his mind somewhere between losing Martine and failing at the Trials. Dr. Black wasn't ready for Jeff's revelations of Bill. That discussion might land him under twenty-four-hour observation and heavy medications. Baltimore would be off the table and he couldn't afford that option.

****

Jeff and Bob were beginning an easy eight-miler through the gardens. On their way out, the two passed a small crowd of teenagers, their movements and body language odd. A football lay discarded in the grass. Jeff nodded to Bob. He stopped his watch and walked to the group. A girl lay in the dark grass, her hair splayed around her. Her eyes were open but lifeless. The sweet smell of grape juice, alcohol, and something else rose from the grass, her sweater stained.

"Has anyone called an ambulance?" Jeff looked to a small girl who nodded, wiping tears. "How long has she been down?"

"A few minutes." She sniffled, hugged by another bystander.

Jeff knelt to check her pulse, his knee slid in muck. Finding no beat, he turned her, pounding her back several times. He probed her mouth finding only small bits of fruit. He looked to Bob. "You know CPR?"

"Just got re-certified at the university."

Jeff pinched the girls nostrils shut and began the four forced breaths. He gagged on the taste of jungle juice and stomach acid on the second and third breath. His breath rattled in her lungs, mixing with her vomit. The break from her mouth was welcomed as Bob began compressions. He was vaguely aware the ambulance had arrived. Men pushed through, moving him aside as they began their work.

"How long have you been resuscitating her?"

"We just started." Jeff wiped his mouth, then spit and wiped again. They cut her purple stained sweater off to reveal her pale, blueish skin. Paddles were placed on her chest.

"How long was she not breathing?"

"I don't know. Several minutes before I got here." Jeff backed to the edge of the circle.

The paddles popped. Her body convulsed. The paddles sounded a second time while another technician ventilated with a hand-held respirator. There was no other sound. The small grassy space felt like a sealed space, a vacuum.

A crow cawed and flapped its wings at the edge of the woods. It's caw drew Jeff's attention. Bill stood beyond the crowd in his raincoat and hat. The two studied each other, oblivious to what was happening between them. Their gaze was interrupted by the girl. She walked slowly to Bill. Jeff looked from the girl standing next to Bill to the lifeless, unresponsive body on the grass. Bill took her hand and whispered, a macabre grandfather helping the child. He smiled, then pointed towards the woods.

"Are you kidding me? I can't believe this." Jeff muttered. Goosebumps ran along his arms and the small hairs on his neck prickled. He met the terrified gaze of the girl, and then the matter-of-fact gaze of Bill. She let go of Bill's hand and walked towards the woods edge, paused, then disappeared. Bill stood alone, hands in pockets. The rancid smell that seemed to follow him, the smell of energy as ghosts came and went filled Jeff's nostrils. Bill tipped his hat and disappeared.

"What did you say?" Bob asked, bringing Jeff back to the real world.

"Nothing. Just an old crow. Come on, let's go. It looks like she's gone."

"Shouldn't we stay to answer questions?"

"Why? She's dead and there is nothing we can do. We did our best."

"How do you know she's gone?"

Jeff pointed to the technicians, packing their gear and preparing her for transport. The kids walked slowly away to various vehicles. The scene was easier to watch than the explanation that he'd seen her leave.

They ran in silence. A girl had died. He'd seen her ghost and it terrified him. To make things worse, he could taste her in his mouth, see her eyes wide with fear, and hear the rattle of fluid in her lungs. It all seemed too fantastic for an easy, eight mile training run.

The two stopped for water at the first fountain. "What are you thinking?" Bob broke their silence.

"You mean the girl? It's a tragedy. She won't graduate or go home to her family tonight. The whole spectacle was horrible and depressing. I could use some Jim Beam right now." He kept the feeling of terror to himself.

Bob switched the subject. "Not to linger on the subject, but what did you do about your coach?"

"I haven't seen him," Jeff lied. "He's on holiday and won't be back until October or November sometime. He gave me all my workouts before leaving."

"Have you figured out what to do when you see him? Catie and I talked. Someone impersonating a dead person is a serious problem. The fact that he has attached himself to you makes it all the more serious. We don't want you to get in trouble."

"Thanks. It helps to have your support. I've told Libby. You're the only three who know. I don't think it's all that serious and I don't want anything to interfere with school or Baltimore. I received my travel documents and entry for the race. I'll confront him when I see him."

They finished at the track, headed for their separate cars. After Bob drove away, Jeff walked across to Bill who waved from the bleachers.

"Good run today?" He said it said it as if nothing strange had occurred.

"The run was easy, but the scene in the gardens not so much. I assume that girl died and that was her ghost?"

"It was her."

"Are you trying to make me believe I'm not cracking up? I have to tell you that it's not working. I'm leaning towards getting the full work up with Dr. Black. Seeing a second ghost only confirms that I need help. All this death is insanity."

"This is real, Jeff. It's completely random and sad that girl died today. It wasn't a good idea for her to drink alcohol and play football with her friends. She died and you did a good thing trying to help her. But since we're linked, you brought me there when you stopped. I showed you what you doubt. You saw her and you know she is as real as I am. I was happy I could help her, too."

"How did you help her?"

"She went where I can't go yet. There was a light for her. I showed her so she could move on. She was a good girl and something bad happened that wasn't her fault. She doesn't have to stay here as I have. I'm still here after all this time. I haven't been able to return home to Baltimore. I think that's where you come in, my boy. You're going to help me get home. I think we're supposed to help each other."

"I'm still pretty shaken up. Trying to help her and touching her lifeless body was bad enough, but seeing her standing next to you is hard to comprehend. There is no one to talk to who would believe what I saw. I need a beer or something stronger to wash away the taste."

Jeff walked to his car in a daze. On one side was reality, the brick building where he studied and the campus grill where he ate. On the other side was the track, a place where only time mattered and that somehow had become a gateway to the spirit world. He searched the empty bleachers, shaking his head.

****

"I need to tell you something." Jeff lay behind Libby with his arm around her tummy. She breathed softly, sleep not far away.

"What?" She yawned.

"I'm sorry but I have to tell someone what happened today."

She grunted. " You told me about the girl. I'm sorry. I want to sleep."

Jeff continued. "I saw another ghost today, the girl in the gardens."

Libby sat up. "Jeff, come on. You didn't see another ghost. I don't even know if I believe you about Bill. I think your stressed and seeing things and it's not funny. You need to go see your doctor tomorrow and have this conversation with her, not me. I can't do this. It's scaring me. I'm sorry you saw someone die. That's traumatic for anyone. But your reaction, seeing something that's not there is not normal. I'm going to sleep. We can talk tomorrow, but I want to hear about your conversation with Dr. Black." Libby laid back down, punched her pillow and rolled over with a final huff.

"I'm glad we had that discussion." Jeff got up and walked into Libby's small kitchen in his briefs. He took the bottle with the brown liquid from the cupboard and poured two fingers into a small glass jar. He sipped then swished the bourbon through his teeth, then gargled a little. The Wild Turkey burned but it wasn't enough. He could still see her eyes and skin, hear the sound of his breath going into her, and taste the effluent from her stomach. He spit into the sink and drank from the faucet.

CHAPTER 13

October

Jeff jogged in place, antsy to start. Breathing deeply, he took in the crisp fall air and city skyline, illuminated by the morning sun. He glanced to his right at the two runners from Boone, rivals from college days. They were fit like him, lean muscle and bone, one tall, one short, both faster than Jeff at the shorter distances in college. Road racing was a different sport and Jeff was a different athlete after the summer of high mileage. The two would provide a good test for Bill's training and maybe a little competition to put some spice in the daily grind. His Sunday training partners jostled behind him, offering encouragement. Jeff nodded to each, sliding past other runners to walk back through the crowd to Libby, a few rows back.

"Good luck, babe." He placed his arms on her shoulders.

"You came back. That's sweet. You got this?"

"Yeah, I got this."

"Better get back up front. Have a good race." They touched foreheads lightly before being separated by the restless pre-race bodies. Jeff took his place in front in the center of the road, trotting out when they called the defending champions name. He turned and waved, smiling broadly, knowing these few moments of recognition were the true wages of the sport. Back on the line, he closed his eyes to clear his mind and took a deep breath.

With a pop from the starter's pistol, the runners surged. Jeff angled to the side to avoid the tangling legs of the young boy's intent on winning the first 100-meters.

Jeff and the Boone runners quickly opened a gap on the field. They ran close behind the motorcycle patrolman, passing the first kilometer just under 3-minutes. Jeff concentrated on form to relax, another day at the office. Race pace always felt challenging, the body never truly ready to exert at higher levels from training. The three left the field behind, heading toward the downtown skyscrapers, making a turn onto Tobacco Row. Monstrous brick warehouses rose up, forming a shaded canyon they slipped down like shadows. Jeff ran third, happy to let the mountain boys set the pace. Leaving downtown for the old Moravian cemetery, they dropped onto the cobbled streets of Old Salem and the College, quickly passing the small park and salt-box homes with colorful doors, lining the way. The pace quickened on the long downhill. A race official called their split-time at halfway, just before the turn up the long hill. It was the designated place where Jeff would make his move. He passed Bill, hard to miss in his signature coat and floppy hat.

"Looking good, Jeff. Push the hill and work the three old maids the last mile."

"It's a kilometer, you stupid ghost," he muttered and took the lead. Jeff pushed the long hill, his body complaining, the other two still in tow. He didn't panic.

They climbed past the 6-kilometer mark. All three rasped for breath approaching the top where the road dipped at the summit, similar to the hills on the capstone run. Jeff relaxed on the downside, then sprinted the first short, steep hill. It was only fifty to sixty-meters but violently steep. He dropped one of his two pursuers going over the first hill. He pushed the second hill, the second runner falling back. His legs burned, but he raced up the third and final hill, the last of the Three Old Maids, so named by his clubmates after a rather severe workout. No one had ever 'busted them.'

"Busted 'em today," Jeff exclaimed, readying for the finish. The road flattened out, just before the last turn and a long, city block to the finish.

The upcoming flat sprint would feel good after the hills. The patrolman's siren announced his arrival with three short blasts to clear the road and open up the path. The finish line was obscured by the turn and the festival crowds.

Jeff moved in effortless, syncopation; his arms matched the movement of his legs. Energy poured from him with plenty to spare. He acknowledged the crowds applause and cheers with a smile and leaned into the turn. With no warning, a woman plowed a baby-buggy directly into his path a few meters ahead. He stepped laterally to avoid the carriage, but his back foot caught on his foreleg as his stride came through, sending him towards the pavement.

"Jeff, no." The startled woman called.

He was lucky his back foot came partially forward, giving him a bit of stability and time for the second foot to come forward, landing in a semi-crouched position, his hands jammed into the pavement. They burned but the pain was minor. He turned to see the tall runner from Boone sprinting towards him, fifty yards and closing. The woman and the baby carriage still blocked part of the road.

"I'm not losing today. Not like this." Jeff hoisted himself like a sprinter coming out of the blocks. His movements were uncoordinated for the first few steps as he lurched into rhythm. He could hear the other runner bearing down, breaths and footsteps. Summoning his remaining energy he moved forward in a makeshift sprint. There would be no victory salutes, no waves to the crowd, and no smiles. Jeff lunged for the line with his eyes shut.

He staggered down the finish shoot then doubled over, his body folded in the familiar post-race position. His hands were slick and slid off his knees from sweat and blood. A race helper touched him with light fingertips and a look of distaste. "Are you OK?" She handed him a towel. His hands stung, but other than that he was okay.

"I'm fine. Did I win?" The fog lifted and he straightened, his breaths slowed.

"Yes, you won. I'll help you to the medical tent for your hands."

Second place congratulated him. "Nice finish. What was that spectator thinking?"

"Thanks. You had a good race, too. I don't know what she was thinking but I'm going to find out." Jeff ducked under the ropes of the shoot, then walked back past the streaming finishers to the scene of the accident and the woman with the stroller now on the sidewalk. He could see Libby racing for the finish. She slowed to a jog when she saw him, surprised to see him walking in the opposite direction. He waved her on.

"I won. Go finish and I'll come find you in a few moments."

He stepped up to the baby carriage and the woman who pushed it. She was as beautiful. Jeff took a deep breath, forgetting Libby, the fall, the win.

"Martine."

"Jeff, I'm so sorry for what happened. When the motorcycle came by, the siren was so loud, I had to move. I wanted to go the other way, but it felt like I was pushed into the street. I must have been jostled by the crowd. I suddenly found myself out there with you sprinting towards us. I just tried to move to the other side of the street as fast as I could." Bill stood behind her, a smug smile. Jeff frowned. "It was such a shock to see you make the turn."

"Stupid ghost," Jeff mumbled.

"What did you say?"

"Nothing, just someone in the crowd."

"I'm sorry. I didn't mean to interfere with your race. I hope you're not mad."

"No, I'm not mad. Things happen, crowds can jostle. Don't worry about it. I just scraped my hands a little and I won." Libby appeared next to Jeff, taking his hand and looking at the damage. "What happened? How come you came up here and didn't wait at the finish?"

"I had a little run-in with the buggy." Jeff motioned. "Libby, this is Martine." She dropped his hand. The look on her face told him how she felt. A crow cawed above them angrily. It wanted the spilled popcorn in the gutter. Crows had not been good omens of late.

"What's she doing here?" Libby looked from Martine to the buggy. "Did you know she was coming to the race?" Her face flooded red. "We need to go. I don't want to stay for awards. Someone else can pick up your trophy."

"I need a couple of minutes to talk with Martine. Is that okay?" Her posture said no. The crow laughed, bobbing up and down.

"Take all the time you want but I'm not staying. I've been waiting since last semester and I won't wait any longer. You can spend all day with her if you want. I'm done with you, her, and your fucking ghosts." Libby quickly walked away, touching her hand to her eyes. A final, "Asshole," was clearly audible as she walked away.

One issue at a time. He turned back to Martine. She was so different from Libby. Her skin fair, complemented by long, raven hair. Her lips curved delicately. She was wearing a wide brim sun hat and sunglasses. Light blue covers stirred in the stroller. The buggy was only a meter in length but created a distance between the two that was immeasurable.

"Jeff, I'm so sorry for everything that just happened."

"It's okay." It wasn't, but he needed to talk to her.

"She's cute. I'm glad you have someone. What did she mean about ghosts?"

"It's a long story. Her name is Libby. She's in class with me." He changed the subject. "I'm surprised to see you. The last time we were together seems so long ago." The memory of the empty apartment, the comforter, and afternoon of sweet goodbyes flooded the space between them.

"That does seem long ago." Her cheeks flushed. "We'll always have that day. A lot has changed since that afternoon." She nudged the stroller. "I needed to get out and decided to come to the festival. I forgot the race was today. Do you remember the last time you and I came? You won that day, too."

"Yeah, I remember. That win came a little easier." Bob and Catie, stopped to say hello, the four had been close before Martine's change of course. Catie leaned in to see the baby. Bob and Jeff made plans to run easy the next day. They said their goodbyes and moved on quickly. Catie patted Jeff's shoulder tenderly.

"You looked good today," Martine continued. "You looked powerful and determined. I'm so glad you were able to get up and finish. How is everything else?"

"Different. I guess that's life. I've changed too. I didn't want to, but sometimes there's no choice. The loss made me more determined to succeed. I'm a bit more jaded about life and people, but I think I needed to toughen up."

"I don't know what you want me to say, Jeff. I told you I was sorry how things ended. I want you to find happiness. Seeing you race brought back good memories when we traveled to races. I've always loved watching you run. I'd like to think I've contributed to your success."

She had contributed; the lonely nights, fragile psyche, a failed suicide. None of that mattered though standing next to her. He brushed the pain aside. If she asked him, he'd stay. He would give up school, running, and anything else if she asked.

Jeff stepped carefully around the stroller to her side to pull on the invisible string that still attached the two. His hand fell to hers on the bar. She didn't move, letting his hand set in hers, their fingers interlocked. His heart leapt. He wanting to caress her face.

"Jeff, why don't you spend the day with us so we can catch up and you can get to know Jackson?" She nodded to the stroller. "I feel so bad about everything that's happened today."

"It's okay; I've taken harder hits."

"What does that mean?" He let her hand go.

"I had a few rough spots last year. It was a difficult year for me."

"It wasn't all wine and roses for me either. Try having a baby." She smiled broadly.

"But you made all the decisions, didn't you?" The smile disappeared.

"Let's not do this here. Be my friend. You can get cleaned up and we can have lunch. It will be like old times."

"Will it? Has anything changed between us, Marti?" He hadn't spoken her name that way for a long time.

She shook her head. "Nothing's changed. I love my life. Teaching is going well and my world revolves around Jackson. I care about you, Jeff. I always will, but I can't go back to us. Your life is athletics and school. My life is teaching and my son. What we had was nice but it's in the past."

"Are you still with Jake?" Jeff pushed forward.

She nodded. "No. We were never going to make it together. But I have met someone and he's very good to me and Jackson." She tended the stroller, tugging at the coverlet. It was obvious that motherhood suited her. "You and I will always be friends. Spend the day with us."

"Enough," He told himself. He was holding onto memories. Their life together was over and had been for some time. It was time to let her go and leave on his terms. "I'm sorry, Marti. I can't be just a friend." Jeff pulled her close, despite his damp, post-race state. She folded against him in the familiar way. He wanted to remember her, for this last touch to last. He smelled her hair and felt the soft skin on her neck with the fine hair.

"Goodbye, Marti."

"Goodbye, Jeff. Don't let her get away. I'm sure she's nice and she runs, too. You two have something in common. You need someone in your life to soften the hard edges from all those miles. Don't make her second to your training log."

"Thanks." He stepped back and lightly touched the pram. Relief swept over him walking away. He'd finished that chapter and other than a few scrapes from the road, he'd come out stronger. He decided to skip the awards and see if he could find Libby. Patching things up would be difficult, a complication as Bill put it. Maybe Bill was right and managing a relationship was too much with school and training. He arrived at an empty parking space. He'd have to run back.

Someone ran behind him, the leather soles of the shoes slapped the pavement. Jeff turned to the man only he could see.

"Jeff, lad, we need to talk. You're going to miss the podium. You've earned it. I want to be there with you when you stand victorious."

"Leave me alone, Bill. We said we'd meet at the track. I can't be seen talking to you here at the festival. I have a lot on my mind."

"But you won, lad, and what a win it was. You had the determination and overcame the fall to win. Now you're in a better place with no distractions. I saw the little girl leave. It will be you and me alone, training for Baltimore. You'll see this is best."

He pictured Bill standing behind Martine, his anger rose. "You caused all of this today, didn't you?"

"I don't know what you're talking about, Jeff. You need to calm down and think things through."

"You pushed Martine into the road. She felt somebody or something push her. She knows what the siren means and would never cross the street that close to the finish. You made her go out there and trip me so the whole big blow-up with Libby and me would occur." He was breathing hard again.

"You need to focus, boy." Bill stood his ground, rocking slightly. "You don't need these women or the doctor. You need to focus on your training and listen to me."

"I don't need a meddling old ghost in my personal life. Now back off. You're the distraction." Jeff shouted, then did as his accounting professor had recommended. He ran like hell.

****

Jeff sat in front of Dr. Black. His foot tapped the floor. Bill would not approve of him being there but he didn't care what the ghost wanted. He had a lot to deal with; an ex-wife, an angry or ex-girlfriend, and coach who was a ghost.

"Can you tell me what's been bothering you? You were unable the last time. You said you needed answers first." She began.

"I still don't have the answers. I need a little time to work some things out.

"So why are you here today?"

"I had a very tough weekend. I ran in the festival race on Saturday. I was 400-meters from the finish when I tripped and fell. I scuffed-up my hands but the hurt was minor. I won." Jeff proudly showed his battle scars, palms out.

"Jeff, I watched it happen."

"You saw me race?"

"I did see you race. You were impressive. My husband said you looked like a well-oiled machine sprinting to the finish. We went for the Bluegrass music and crafts but stopped to watch the race. We were standing just before the corner where you fell. I don't know what that woman with the stroller was thinking."

"You should have introduced yourself. We could have had a session there on the street corner. That was Martine and her baby. They came to the festival, too. Someone in the crowd shoved her, so our reunion was unexpected."

"I had no idea. Talk about a small world. We watched you fall and I admire your resilience. What drove you to get up and finish? Weren't you in pain?"

"That's what I do. I finish. It hurt a little but I was lucky to land as I did. I only scraped my hands a little. I didn't notice the pain at that moment. I had to finish and I had to win. I wasn't going to let victory escape me."

"How would you have felt if the win had escaped you and you'd finished second or not been able to finish at all?"

"None of those things happened and I did win. I've had to deal with loss before, some of my doing and some not of my doing. It doesn't feel good either way. That's why I couldn't let this one get away." Jeff picked at the scab on his hand. "Did you see what happened after that?"

"No, we went to the music pavilion after you crossed the line."

"I walked back to Martine and Libby followed me."

"How did that turn out?"

"How do you think?" Jeff shook his head. "Libby gave me an ultimatum to leave with her and I hesitated. She stormed off and hasn't returned my calls. She's been avoiding me in class. A friend told me she left our study group."

"What will you do?"

"I have to talk to her at some point and apologize. She wanted me to choose her, to leave with her, but I needed to speak to Martine. I don't know how I feel. I mean I know I care about Libby but it's all a bit much right now after seeing Martine. Libby wants me to commit, and my coach wants her gone."

"Tell me about Martine? How was it seeing your ex-wife?"

"She looked lovely and I found it easy to want our old, familiar comfort. I could have spent the day with her believing there was a chance to reconcile. If she asked me to come back to her I would have done anything she asked. I would have given everything up even though I knew it wouldn't last and the devastation that would follow."

"So, what happened?"

"She shared where her life is now and I could see I'm no longer a part of it. My obsession with her is over. I held on as long as I could but all she wanted was friendship. I could finally see that and I'm not capable of being only a friend. I told her that wouldn't work for me and said goodbye. I walked away and it's funny because I expected to feel pain, sadness, longing, but there wasn't any. I felt relief because I didn't want her new life. I only wanted our old life. I'm okay moving on. I guess you could say I crossed that finish line, too."

"That's a big breakthrough."

"There's one less ghost in my life."

"That's a strange way to put it but it sounds healthy, moving on. How are things with your coach?"

"Not well at the moment. Bill didn't want me seeing Libby, either. He's happy as can be that it's just the two of us now. Quite frankly he pisses me off, maybe because he's right. There is other stuff, too, I can't talk about yet."

"Maybe you two should part ways? Your interactions don't sound healthy."

"He's just old and he's old-school about training and racing. He wants no distractions. I promised him I'd see this through our marathon in December. It will be good when that race is over and we go our separate ways. Then I can concentrate on exams and take some time off from training."

"Will you have the answers you need and be able to talk about what's bothering you?"

"I hope so. It will feel good to get the race and semester exams out of the way. I'm looking forward to the break and the rest."

"That timeline sounds like it should work. Your training has been relentless. It will be good for your mind to rest as well as your body. You mentioned going home for Thanksgiving and Christmas. Has anything changed? You were upset with your father the last time we had a session."

"No, nothing's changed. Libby and I talked about spending the holidays together but that's not going to happen now. I guess I need to try to get along with my father, at least for the sake of my mother and the holiday."

"Will your father go to the race?"

"He was always good about going to my races as a boy. But we are two different people. He's right brained and quantitative. I'm left brained and qualitative."

"How will you make it work?"

"My run-in with Martine taught me something about myself. I have to make these decisions in my life. It's up to me to show him who I am. If he doesn't accept me, then it's on him and there's not much I can do about that. I'm hoping we can talk and have a happy holiday."

****

Jeff stretched near the track fence, the air cool in the late October afternoon. The easy seven-miler would soon be in his journal. Bill walked up tentatively.

"Have you recovered from the race?"

"Most of the soreness is gone." Jeff studied his hands. "I'm glad I wasn't hurt, no thanks to you. That fall could have been catastrophic and then where would we be?"

"I wouldn't let that have happened, lad."

"You have no right to mess with my personal life. And once again, what is it with you and your obsession with women in my life. You pushed Martine out in front of me. I might have hurt her and the baby. I also might have run right by and never seen her there. Libby and I would have still been together. She's been a big comfort to me and I miss her."

"I didn't do much. I just," Bill paused for a second, choosing his words. "I just helped the girl decide to cross the street."

"How'd you do that?"

"Just a little trick, getting inanimate things to move. I helped her take the first step, so you'd meet. I wouldn't have let you get hurt, and you did the rest by going back to speak to her in front of your girlfriend."

"You are such an ass. I don't need the drama and I don't need you."

"You're right, you don't need the drama and now it's gone. All you have to do is run, stay focused and prepare to race. Then I will leave you and you can live your life as you see fit. I will get you to the starting line in one piece. Are we on the same page?"

Jeff nodded reluctantly. "Why, Bill? Why do you need me to run in Baltimore?"

"I can't say with any certainty but I need to get back. It's been a long time since I was able to be home. Both you and I are supposed to be at that race."

"I'm nothing more than a ticket to Baltimore, am I?"

"In a manner of speaking, yes, you're my ticket home. That's where I need to be if I'm to have any peace. We have an agreement. Just focus on staying fit. Keep warm so you don't get sick. Let's plan on some faster running and one last race. The dual meet next month should do. You'll be ready at that point."

"The team is running quarters this week. I thought I might run with them for speed work. Rob and George are running well so I'll work with them.

Jeff began to walk away. He stopped and turned back to Bill. " I still have reservations about this arrangement. How do I know this isn't all in my mind?"

"You don't. Stick to your plan, lad." Bill began to fade, his form gauzy in the late afternoon light.

Jeff stared in disbelief. "I hate it when he does that."

CHAPTER 14

Jeff, Rob, and George walked to the line, grim with determination for the work they'd subject their bodies to over the next forty minutes. All three knew the workout, posted on the locker room cork board earlier in the week: twenty, 400-meter repeats. They would run 5-miles at slightly faster than race pace with minuscule rest intervals, a staple workout for any distance runner. The simulation adapted their bodies to sustained running in an anaerobic state. Matt held the watch, directing their efforts while Randy did the same for the shorter distance guys jogging on the far side of the track.

"On my whistle," Matt clicked the watch on the shrill blast.

Jeff led the first lap with George and Rob locked behind him. The three galloped around the track, the first lap covered in 72-seconds. Jeff felt a little stiff on the first lap. The feeling was familiar, a combination of the cumulative work from the previous days work and muscles that needed more warm, oxygen rich blood to work better. The 100-meter recovery jog went by quickly. Reaching the white line, Matt blew the whistle again. Rob led with Jeff, and George, just behind. They finished the second lap in 72-seconds again, taking tiny, tip-toe steps to lengthen the precious recovery jog.

The three continued the workout without talk, determined to hit their times. The interval times dropped; 72 for the first set of four, 71 for the second set, and 70-seconds for the third. The next to last set averaged

68-seconds, their bodies warm and ready for the pace work. The tell-tale burning in his neck arteries indicated lactic acid, the by-product of the effort coursing through his blood vessels as the laps added up. There were four left. Jeff did his job, holding the pace back, a steady 68-seconds.

"Good one, Jeff. Keep it right there, perfect pace." Matt called from across the track.

Rob brought the next lap around in 66. "Easy, boys easy, no racing," Matt yelled. They jogged their hundred meters a little slower, in anticipation of the second-to-last lap. George led with Rob on his shoulder and Jeff just behind, careful with his closeness to keep the undergrads reigned in. The three rounded the last curve, three abreast and crossed the line together.

Matt snapped the watch, "66-seconds. Hold it down for the last one, I don't want any racing." That would be difficult. Their muscles and lungs burned, but all three could easily run the last in 65-seconds or faster. The rest of the team had completed their shorter, faster training and gathered in small groups of two or three to cheer as they warmed down.

"I'll take the last one." Jeff nodded to Matt. The trio lined up. The whistle blasted.

Jeff led around the curve with George and Rob tucked behind, holding back, his stride lengthening as the trio entered the back straight. Rob went by in a flash and led into the final turn. Jeff let the undergrad go, easing off the gas to keep Matt and Randy happy and do the work. Rob led with George on his shoulder and Jeff just behind. The three came down the final straight single file and a stride apart. Matt called out 66-seconds, the workout complete.

"Good job, I'll come with you for your warm down," Matt called. He deposited his pad and stopwatch with Randy. The two had a brief conversation before he jogged over.

They ran slowly through the woods for a well-deserved, three miles warm down. The soft dirt and pine needle trail provided relief for their tight tendons and distressed muscles. Jeff and Matt ran behind the two undergraduates.

"Thanks for holding back on that last one."

"No problem, I'm happy to help the guys and 66 was plenty fast. I needed that workout to clean the cylinders."

"You talk to Libby yet?"

"I haven't had time, and I'm not so sure it's the right time for us with everything going on right now."

"What do you mean?"

"The marathon's coming up soon, and I want to focus on a good effort. I'll see my family over the holidays and I hope that goes well and then exams. I'm not so sure it's the right time for Libby and me to work things out. I need to get a few things settled."

"I heard you ran into Martine. How did that go?"

"It was okay. Martine's different and I'm different. I guess we've moved on and each of us has other priorities now. Time heals all wounds and I was able to walk away with no regrets."

"I'm sure that was hard, saying goodbye to her and having your girlfriend walk away all in a few minutes time. Life sucks sometimes."

"You know, Matt, I'm okay. I'm running great and I'm healthy. The only thing that matters right now is December's marathon, then finish the semester and enjoy some time with my family. Maybe things will be different for Libby and me next semester. We'll see."

The runners exited the woods onto the practice field. Matt stopped Jeff as they walked toward the locker room.

"Randy asked to see you before you leave today."

"What does he want?"

"Don't know, but he wants me there, too."

"Anything I should worry about?"

"He didn't say."

Matt and Jeff walked into the small office on the third floor. One wall featured shelves full of books on history, literature, and track and field. The opposite wall had a large window that overlooked the track complex.

Randy greeted the two from his desk. "Hey, Jeff, Matt. Thanks for coming up. You looked good out there today, Sport."

"Those two are in great shape. I'll be excited to see how they race at conference and nationals."

"Conference will be exciting and Rob has a good chance to win depending on Clemson's Dutchmen. I'm sure your anxious to get home but I need to talk with you about your training. What do you see out my window?"

Jeff peered into the dusk at the track and bleachers. He had an idea what might come next.

"The track and bleachers."

"I've seen you out there lately when I leave at night. You've been carrying on quite the animated conversation, by yourself. What's going on, Sport?"

"I'm working things out." He had a bad feeling about where the conversation might be going. "My marriage, my relationship with Libby, school and home. It helps to talk things out like I do with my counselor."

"What about your coach?" Randy handed a piece of paper to Jeff. "A friend at Maryland dug this up. I asked him to look up Bill Atlee at the university library. He's quite the legend in Maryland and still has a few records. He's also dead. My friend sent that clipping, an obituary from 1954. I also looked up the Runners World issue when he made the Hall of Fame a few years back. You're race results were in that issue. I need you to tell me what's going on."

Jeff sat silently on the small sofa, gazing out the large window at the track he had recently navigated so well. It was ironic how easy the workout had gone and how difficult the conversation had become. The absurdity made him chuckle.

"This isn't funny, Sport. I think you've made all this up and I'm not sure why. Did you pick him because of the magazine. Did you pick him because he died and you didn't think anyone would check? Is it school, your family, or your relationships that are causing you to create this crazy story? What would make you do this?"

"He's real, whoever he is. He sounded legitimate when he approached me about coaching and I should have checked more into his background.

I haven't seen him in a while so I don't have an answer for you. I believed him, and he is real. He's not made-up."

"Jeff, I talked to Dr. Black."

"She can't talk to you about me. She has to keep what I tell her confidential."

"Take it easy, Sport. I called Dr. Black and told her I'm concerned about you. I set you up with her last year, remember? She can get you whatever help or medication you need from the hospital and her attending physician. I wanted her to know that I am concerned. If you want, I can call your family, talk to the Dean of the graduate school, or anyone else you wish so you can clear your schedule."

"I don't need to clear my schedule. I told Dr. Black I would come in after the race before semester break."

"This can't wait. I think you need a full evaluation and if Dr. Black feels you need it, then medication. I've been in athletics and the university a long time. I know the signs when someone is troubled. I can't risk having you around the team, not like this."

"Like what?"

"Like hallucinations. A grown person having hallucinations can be dangerous to himself and those around them. I've seen you sitting by yourself, night after night, talking to no one. I think your coach is a charade."

"I'm not hallucinating. I'm working things out. I found it helped to talk about training, school, and my relationships. It's no different than when I talk to Dr. Black or when I'm up on the ladder painting houses. You know that, Matt."

"I didn't know you were having conversations up there."

"I don't want to do this, Jeff, but I think you are a danger to yourself and the team," Randy said. "I'm taking away your athletic privileges until Dr. Black clears you. Empty out your locker and turn in your key to Matt. I'm sorry, Sport."

Randy's declaration stung. Jeff fumbled, trying to hang onto his cozy world. Bill was right about Dr. Black and now Randy. They would take everything away. If he did it their way, he'd be on heavy medication and stuck with a ghost forever. He needed to finish.

"Can I run in the cross-country dual with the track club in November? That's my last race before the marathon. I'll stay away from the track and the guys until then."

"I'm sorry Sport, but no. I can't have the liability to the school or the team. You're out for now. Please listen to us and get help. I don't think racing is healthy for you right now. There are more important things in your life, namely, your mental health. Get help, get well, and come back out in the spring."

Jeff walked out with Matt. "This is surreal. I meet a guy who turns out to be dead or isn't who he says he is and everything I care about starts to fall apart."

"What's going on, Jeff? You're one of the most normal guys I know. I don't have to worry about you of all my tenants. Nothing about this makes sense. Tell me what's going on so I can help you."

"I'm tired, Matt. The workout and discussion with Randy wore me out. Do me a favor and talk to coach. See if he will relent and let me race. It's the last hard effort before the marathon. I'll see you later. I need to be alone for a while."

"Call me if you need to talk. I'll be back at the house."

****

Jeff's chin rested on his hands. A half-full mug of beer and a full shot glass with amber liquid sat six inches away. He downed the shot, warm on his throat, chased by the cold beer. He pushed the empty mug back, signaling for another round to the bartender.

"Dillon, what are you doing here? I've never seen you at Ziggy's before." George and some of the cross-country guys gathered around, his presence at the college pub newsworthy.

"Felt I needed a change of scenery to work some things out." He'd started the night at Penelope's, across the street, but left when Libby arrived with one of his classmates.

"We heard about you getting banned. What happened? Randy must have been pissed about something."

"I can't say and I'm not supposed to be around you guys, so I can't hang out. There's something you can do for me, George. I need you to work on Randy so I can race in the dual?"

"No problem, Dillon. Rob and I want to kick your butt, anyway. We'll get you eligible again." He clapped his back and laughed. "See you later." The boys headed to the foosball tables.

Jeff downed the shot and stacked the small glasses. He slowly gulped his beer, putting his chin back on his folded hands.

A second hand slapped his back, the touch cold. "Being shoved aside doesn't feel very good, does it? One moment you're winning and the hero and the next you're damaged goods and a liability. No one cares about all you've achieved. I know."

Bill's arrival didn't surprise him. He shivered from the touch. "Bill, is this all a bad dream? I won the race but I didn't get to enjoy the victory. I lost Libby and she may be with someone else now. I'm banned from the cross-country team because I can't explain you. It's hopeless right now." The cold spread from Bill's hand down his arm, the bar suddenly blurry. "Whoa, I think I've had enough," Jeff put both hands down to steady himself.

"There was no hope. I couldn't take it any longer." Bill's voice sounded muted.

Jeff opened his eyes, surprised to see the bartender, an older man with a long sleeve white shirt, bow-tie, and curled, handlebar mustache. He had replaced the young woman from Ziggy's with her torn tee-shirt and tats. The bar was different too; longer and made of highly polished wood. He could smell sawdust from the floor. A large silver cup sat across from Jeff, the centerpiece in front of a big mirror with a picture of a young man breaking the tape. A much younger Bill sat next to him, his jacket dirty. He knocked back a whiskey then accepted a beer from the willowy barmaid. Her finger rand down his as he accepted the mug, the two sharing a smile.

Footsteps clomped on the floorboards. "Look at 'im boys. He stares at that cup like it's a bleeding icon and him the Blessed Mother." The group laughed. "Hey Billy-boy, buy your crew a round of drinks. You won all that money racing. Oh, that's right, you didn't win a penny, just a few fancy shoes. You ran further than a horse, and what did it get ya' but a pair of creaky old knees? You're a loner, Billy-boy and we don't like loners on the crew. You snuck off today without lettin' us know. I think he's here sniffing around that pretty little bird behind the bar. One at home isn't enough, our Bill wants a second, boys." The group laughed louder. "Maybe we need a second? Want to share her with the gang, Billy-boy?"

Bill tensed. A hand clasped his shoulder. He swung around with fists curled and rose to the challenge. "What I do in my own time is my business. Now go away."

He faced a young man in a black suit and white collar. "Leave him alone, boys. Order us a round and get the darts ready. I'm buying tonight." The boys walked off laughing loudly, the last impersonating Bill with an exaggerated, high-knee jog.

"They're right, you know. Staring at that cup isn't doing you any good and cheap whiskey won't give you any answers." The priest pushed the shot glasses away. Bill glanced at the young woman pouring the round of beers. "She's not the answer either, Bill." The priest drew Bill's gaze.

"I don't know what to do, Father. Everything has become so complicated and I'm so tired that I can't think straight. How did life end up this way?"

"You have everything to live for, Bill. You're just in a dark place and need to find the good in life."

"It's humiliating, to work with that crew at the Point. I don't mind the work but the men and the bosses are relentless. They treat me like a circus animal."

"I'm sure it isn't as bad as all that. It's good, honest labor and there is honor in that, son."

"I was an Olympian. I won races and now I'm nobody. I'm just a number that pounds steel every day. Those boys are right, where did all that running get me?"

"No one said life was easy, lad. You made choices. You chose to run and it took you places. The times are hard and we can't control any of that."

"I had to work. I had to help my family during the depression. I couldn't go to school, and I wasn't any good at the books anyway. Running and winning was the only relief in a world of drudgery, slinging newspapers for four hours each day."

"We know you did well running. You can be proud of those accomplishments." They both looked to the big silver cup and the picture of Bill breaking the tape that hung on the bar's wall. "You have a beautiful wife and boys, the real reward in life. I baptized those lads, and they need you. You should be home with them right now, not here drinking cheap whiskey and chasing the barmaid." She smiled, nodding to the priest and Bill, her apron tight on her belly. "I want you to go home and take care of your family. They're what's important."

Bill stood with the young priest's help. "I'm sorry, Father. I feel so helpless, and I don't know what to do."

"Go home, Bill. You worry me. You'll find all the hope you need in those three beautiful faces at home and they will find the same in yours. Come and see me on Saturday after confession and we'll talk then. Now off with you."

Bill walked out the door and stopped, looking back to the priest and then the woman who wiped down the bar. The grip on Jeff's shoulder relaxed. Jeff opened his eyes, greeted by the familiar environs of Ziggy's. Bill stood beside him.

"I know about hopelessness, lad. It's no way to live. You have to be stronger than all of this, losing the girl, losing your spot with the team, your father. I let it get to me, but you can't."

"Leave my father out of this. We agreed that you have no say outside of training. He's all I have and I'll decide how I interact with him."

"All I'm saying is we're in the last phase of your training, so you have to be careful. No missteps, no injury, and no getting drunk." Bill pushed the mug away from Jeff. "I know it stings right now but you can get through this. Run easy the next two days and then we'll plan the rest of your schedule. We'll do your fast runs in the gardens away from the track and the team. The soft surface will be good for your legs." Jeff nodded. "Now it's time for you to go home. You're in no condition to drive."

"Are you going to drive me, BIll?" Jeff laughed. Bill remained stoic, an annoyed look crossed his face. "They think I'm hallucinating and maybe I am. I don't know what to do."

Jeff asked the bartender for the phone and dialed Matt's number. "Hey, it's Jeff. I'm at Ziggy's. Can you pick me up?" He hung up and placed his chin back in his hands.

CHAPTER 15

November

The days turned cold. Jeff shoved gloves in his hoody's kangaroo pocket. His marathon preparation was coming to an end, the long miles tapering for shorter runs at a faster pace to sharpen his speed. Running took on an added intensity with tempo runs of three and six miles followed by shorter sprints in the garden to hone his speed. Jeff executed the workouts alone, flying along the garden paths. Classes also began to wrap-up. He prepared for final exams and final project presentations after the Thanksgiving holiday.

Jeff sat across from Matt in the darkened booth. Matt worked on ribs, pausing to wipe the sticky, Carolina-style sauce from his face and fingers. Jeff opted for the less messy, though somewhat greasier pulled pork sandwich.

"Any word from Randy on me running in the dual meet?"

"There is. Randy's going to let you run with the track club. Rob and George convinced him they need you in the race to push them. He wants you to set a fast pace to simulate conference and nationals and get them used to the tempo. The ban on using the other athletic facilities and working out with the team is still in place until your doctor clears you. But you can run in the dual meet."

Jeff high-fived his friend despite Matt's sauce-covered fingers. Jeff passed him one of the little foil covered packets from the bowl on the table.

"That's great news. I've dropped my mileage and have a lot of pent-up energy. I need to race."

"I'm glad it worked out. Take it easy on my guys. Remember, you're there to pace them."

"Loud and clear, coach." Jeff popped a hushpuppy into his mouth.

"Are you going home for Thanksgiving?"

"I'll only be there for the weekend. It will be good to see my folks. I'm also going to run the course while I'm home. I have to get back to work on Mason's marketing class project. We have to present an advertising campaign when we get back from break. Dr. Mason and Robert Flynn of Flynn & Flynn Advertising, will grade the projects."

"I know Flynn, he's a good guy. He was in my frat and runs the occasional road race. You've probably seen him or he's seen you at races."

"My group still needs a concept. We have to design a promotional campaign for suntan lotion. We've got our first creative meeting this afternoon. Hopefully, we'll think of something before we all leave for the holiday."

Matt read the newspaper while Jeff piled the trash on a tray. He picked up one of the cleansing packets to remove the grease from each finger. He then picked up a second unopened packet and held it up. Jeff studied the wipe. "I wonder?" He stuffed a handful in his book bag. Matt's laughter brought his focus back to the booth.

"*Doonesbury?* What's going on today?"

"Zonker just won the George Hamilton Cocoa-Butter Open, the suntan world championship. Hey, why don't you get him as your suntan lotion spokesperson? Everyone reads *Doonesbury*. That would be cool."

"That's brilliant. Mind if I borrow the comics for the meeting later?" He tucked the newspaper in his bag with the wipes. "Tell Randy thanks and let him know I won't go bat-shit-crazy during the race."

****

Race day dawned cool and damp, perfect cross-country weather. The meet was low-key, a chance for the college boys to tune up for the conference championship. For Jeff it was a final test, a chance to blow out the pipes and deal with the pent-up anxiety of the upcoming marathon. The rain held off though the clouds hung low and jagged. It could start at any moment. Jeff warmed up with an easy jog through the wooded trails, then sat under the medical tent to stretch. He watched the women's team finish, the old-gold and black clad girls took the top seven places easily. They then gathered in a tight circle, shoulder to shoulder, and sang the alma mater to the boys, their season complete while the rest of the field, a few unattached runners and the community college girls, ran in, dodging the victory celebration. A few spots of rain fell while the theme song from *Chariots of Fire* and *St. Elmo's Fire*, blared from the speakers. The music was a little much for the low-key meet, Jeff mused.

The whistle called the twenty-some runners to the start; a mostly stomped-out white line on the wet turf. Jeff stuffed his rain-suit in his bag under the tent, jogging to the starting grid. He took his place in the chalk line box next to his club mates; Bob, Ed, Bill and Larry all jogged in place. They had just enough for a scoring team, leaving work early to race. Larry was chatting nervously and made no sense at all.

Ed shook his head impatiently. "Shut up, Larry." The random chatter became more animated. Jeff smiled.

Matt walked up to check on the university boys. Rob and George stood next to Jeff with the others spread across the line.

Matt nodded to Jeff. "You're the rabbit so run fast but don't burn-out my guys." Matt then leaned over to Rob and George, his comment just loud enough for Jeff to hear. "Kick his ass."

Jeff met his gaze. There would be an ass-kicking, though he would not be the victim.

"Ready to give it a go, Rob?"

"Let's do this," he answered. The two fist bumped. The rain began in earnest, a few drops at first, then solid rain followed by sheets. It was difficult to make out the far post where they would turn for the shelter of the woods. Steam rose from the warm, closely packed bodies.

The music died. Randy walked to midfield. He wore a hat much like Bill's and a big poncho over his warm-ups. "Have a good run today, guys.

It's going to be slick, so watch your footing. There will be one command. Runners set, followed by the gun." He held the bullhorn to his mouth and raised the gun skyward. "Runner's set." The gun popped.

Jeff raced for the far side pole, careful to stay in front of the sharp spikes of the college boy's that ran close on his heels. Jeff wore rubber cleated flats, not taking any chances with injury and the marathon looming. He rounded the marker first with Rob and George in tow and the field strung out behind.

After a quick lap around the field, the course ducked into the woods. The tall pines would provide shelter from the drenching rain, the pine needle path soft and aromatic. The faster tempo felt good after the week of rest. Jeff came up on the first mile in 4-minutes, 45-seconds; fast but comfortable. The path led them to the back of the small forest and a short hill before it looped back to the start. Jeff, George, and Rob had separated from the pack and passed the second-mile marker. Jeff attacked the small hill. It took a few moments to climb before the steep drop-off on the back and the return to the flat forest floor. Jeff and the two collegians passed their teammates, headed towards the exit from the woods and the second lap. Jeff broke into the open, pelted by the rain. Rob followed a stride behind with George another few strides back. Matt ran beside the first two as they circled the slick, grassy field. He felt good, despite the cold rain on his face and chest.

"Good pace, Jeff," Matt shouted. "Hang on, Rob, push the second loop." He stopped to catch his breath and exhort George. "Get back up with those two, Georgie."

Jeff had control of the race and could feel the separation from the two collegians. The trio reentered the woods, the only sound their rapid, hoarse breaths. Jeff sprinted to the top of the small hill for the second time without any let-up on the downside, his arms wide for balance as his heels dug in the pine needles.

"Stay with me, Rob," Jeff rasped.

Rob didn't respond but he could hear him laboring a few steps behind. The two raced alone through the pines, eager for the grass field and finish line. Jeff exited the woods in a higher gear. He sprinted across the grass to open a small gap and take the win. The time flashed on the clock, 24-something, sub-5 minute pace; good on a sloppy day. Rob came across a few seconds later, spent. He was covered in Jeff's kicked-up mud. Looking down, Jeff noticed his shins and shorts were just as speckled. The two stood in the shoot, arms on each other's shoulders for support. There were no words spoken, both reveling in the effort and luxurious rest. They waited for George. Steam rose from their backs in the cool, wet air. George exited the woods with a noticeable limp. He jogged across the finish. Jeff and Rob helped him to the trainer's tent. The rest of the field struggled to the finish in twos and threes; Stevie, Rick, Whitey, Layne, and Darryl. They summoned their sprints for the final few yards. The college men took the next seven spots after Jeff, followed by the community college runners and then the track club; Will, Bob, Ed and finally Larry, his finishing kick less dramatic. Jeff cheered from the wood's edge, soaked by the rain.

The warm-down was an easy loop in the woods. Larry provided play-by-play of the battle up-front between Jeff and Rob. "He's got a shot to win conference and will probably go to NCAA's and you just beat him. You must be in some shape, Dillon."

"Rob deserves credit in these conditions, but honestly, I felt I could have run another five at that pace."

"It looks like you're ready for Baltimore," Bob added.

"Yeah, I feel good. I think I am ready. I'll take it easy through Thanksgiving then fly out the following week."

After the warm down, Jeff parted from his clubmates and stopped by the trainer's tent to check on George. "How's he feeling?"

"George is finished for the season," Randy stated. "It's his knee. You looked good today, an easy run through the woods. I'm sure you'll do well in Baltimore. Call me when you get back and let's get everything taken care of so you can come back and work with the team."

"Thanks, I will. I appreciate you letting me run today. Good luck at Conference. Rob's ready." Jeff waited for everyone to leave the field sitting in his car, impatient and soggy. He checked the area to make sure he was alone then walked to the edge of the woods. Rain dripped from the trees while his shoes splashed through puddles from the earlier deluge. For once Bill was dressed appropriately in his raincoat and hat, though his outward appearance was thin and vaporous.

"Good race, Jeffrey. You ran very efficiently. You are ready."

"Thanks, it felt easy. I'm going home for Thanksgiving for a few days. Are there any special workouts you want me to run?"

Big drips fell from the brim of his hat. "I'm going with you. I can give them to you there when we run the course."

"Oh great. Look who's coming home for Thanksgiving. Should I have my mother set an extra place at the table? You know the coach thinks I've lost my marbles. Do we need to include my family? I don't want my parents to know their son sees ghosts."

"Take it easy. You won't even know I'm there. You're the only one who can see me."

"You look different tonight. Are you fading?"

"Our link is weak. You don't have much pain anymore, do you?"

"No, I don't. I feel pretty damn good right now with my running, school, and family. Is this how this works? Will you just fade into nothing if all the pain goes away?"

"I will eventually fade and I won't be visible unless you want to see me. I found you at your worst after your marriage fell apart. You didn't work, you didn't run, you just drank and slept. I watched you struggle. We met at your biggest race, another low point. I waited for a long time to be able to talk to you. I'll still be with you, you just won't see much of me. I need to get to Baltimore, as we agreed. I want to go home."

"I understand, I think. I'm feeling good and energized and you're diminishing. I'm sorry. You've helped me a great deal and I am grateful. I've enjoyed getting to know you. It's too bad this has to be so weird and complicated. I'm in a field at night talking to a ghost in the mud." Both laughed. "I better get dried off and warm. I'll see you later."

Bill waved, his body shimmered and faded. Ozone wafted in the heavy night air.

****

Jeff opened the door quietly to slip into a back-row seat. Dr. Bailey turned slowly towards the noise, an eyebrow arched. He went back to the board. "And the corresponding debit." He made a thick white mark under the word. A similar mark underlined the word 'credit.' Jeff was 15 minutes late for his last class before break. He hadn't missed a thing judging by the mournful expressions of his classmates.

He hung back when class ended.

"Did you have a good run this morning, Mr. Dillon?"

"I'm sorry, Dr. Baily. It wasn't a run, I just overslept. I raced yesterday and was more tired than I thought."

"No worries. You're doing fine in class. How is your mystery coming? Your haunting as I recall?"

"I'm still experiencing it, but I hope it will be over soon."

"Jeff, let's take a walk. Some things are better said outdoors under the sun."

The two stepped out onto the quad. They stuffed hands in pockets and snugged their coats in the brisk breeze. The two walked on the circular brick sidewalk under the hardwoods, stripped of fall leaves and replaced by toilet paper from the last football victory celebration.

"I've been concerned about your story about seeing ghosts."

"You haven't talked to anyone about what I shared have you? Things could get difficult if word got out."

"I wouldn't do anything without talking with you first. I'm worried however. When a person under stress starts to see things unnatural or supernatural, it's usually a cause for alarm. You're under stress just being in this program, much less training and racing at a national level. I'm not saying I don't believe you but it's not normal. It's easier to believe what you're experiencing is caused by illness or something else that's tangible."

They sat on the steps of the Chapel. Their discussion seemed small against the brilliance of the day and stately brick columns.

"I confided in you because I needed to tell someone. Someone who wouldn't judge me or try to tell me I'm crazy. It's so difficult to deal with a ghost, a real ghost that haunts me. I didn't ask for this to happen. I was in a very low place last January before I met Libby. The ghost picked up on my depression. He'd committed suicide many years ago. Since that time, I've become stronger and happier while he's become weaker. I think we'll part soon so he can rest. I know this sounds far-fetched and I'm not asking you to believe me. It helps to be able to confide in someone."

"I don't judge and unless you show bizarre behavior you don't need to worry. The part about the suicide is troubling." They were both silent and stared onto the quad. He lit his pipe, releasing a mouthful of fragrant smoke.

"Don't worry, Dr. Bailey. That is something he did, not me. I want to go home and see my family. I want to race. I want to pass exams. That's my focus."

"Let me tell you a story, Jeff. When I was in Vietnam I had five friends cut-down in front of me. We were ambushed." He paused to remember, sucking on the pipe with short breaths to draw the smoke. He blew a long plume out. "It was a routine mission and we weren't expecting anything to happen. I was young and a total mess after that incident. It took years to get over."

"I'm sorry."

"It's okay, now. The night terrors have stopped. What I wanted to tell you is that my friends still visit me every night. This took place a long time ago, but I see their faces when I sleep, sometimes when I'm awake. I've gotten used to having them with me. I would miss them if they ever left. I pray they're at peace. You could say I'm haunted, too. I think all of us are haunted some way or another. Who's to say what's real, what's a memory or a ghost?"

"That must have been hard, seeing those men, your friends for all these years. My ghost is just a poor spirit who needs to get home. I think my task is to help him. Did I tell you he was a runner? He ran the Olympic Marathon in 1928. I'm hoping after the race in Baltimore that he can rest and so can I."

"That's pretty bizarre, the ghostly Olympian, but I won't judge you. You see what you see and we all need to rest at some point, especially when the past haunts us." They stood, stiff from the chill of the brick steps. He banged his pipe gently on the column to empty the ashes.

"Thanks for the talk, Dr. Bailey. It helps that you listen and don't judge. And please don't worry. I feel great and I'm ready to race in Baltimore. I hope you have a nice holiday. Will you stay or will you go somewhere in the Airstream?"

"You can find me with the trout, high in the Appalachians. Wish me luck."

CHAPTER 16

The drive home to Baltimore for Thanksgiving was uneventful and a chance to reconsider everything that had happened since May. Jeff negotiated the normal heavy traffic around the DC Beltway, oddly comforted by the efforts of humanity trying to get home just like him. He pulled into the long driveway, welcomed by the house he had left to go to school years before. The house smelled of pastry and fall spices, his mother in full bakery mode. Several pies were in development on the counter and kitchen table with fillings on the stove.

"Momma." Her expression brightened. She held her floured hands up as he embraced her.

"Jeffrey, you're home. You're so thin."

"I'm just in good shape."

"Can I make you a sandwich?"

"Not right now."

"I'm so glad you're here. I've looked forward to this holiday. Would you like something to drink?" She waved a half-filled highball glass. Holiday music played in the background. "A little holiday cheer?"

"No. I'm going to run later. Can I help you?" Jeff went to the drawer for an apron, washed his hands, and began to roll out a dough ball. His mother refreshed her drink from the Seagram's and 7-Up bottles on the counter.

"Your father will be happy to see you. We get lonely, just the two of us." She sipped while Jeff worked the dough. "I was sorry it didn't work out for you to bring your new friend home."

"Her name is Libby. Things have been difficult for us lately. We haven't had time to talk. Maybe we can talk before semester break."

"It would be nice to have a full house. Have you heard from," she took a swallow, "Martine?"

"I saw her a few weeks ago. She's doing well and she's happy."

"I always hoped you two would reconcile. I know it might not be appropriate for me to say but I miss her. She was the daughter I never had." His mother refilled her glass, the brown bottle covered in flour fingerprints. "I enjoyed having a daughter."

"I miss her too, Mom. But we are both happy with our lives and it's not going to work out for us. I'm sorry. Are you feeling okay?"

"It has been hard. I was looking forward to being a grandmother for the holidays this year. I wanted to set the table for five." She sighed, sitting down on a chair.

"You know the baby wasn't mine."

"It didn't matter to me. I would have loved your children however they came into this world."

"I told her the same thing when we parted." Jeff went to his mother, putting his arms around her. "It didn't matter to me either. It only mattered that she came home to start over. But she chose another life and we've both moved on. I'm excited about the future, focusing on my studies and the upcoming race."

She slumped in her chair, her hand lose around the glass. "I think I need to rest for a while. Do you mind if I take a nap? All the preparation has worn me out." Jeff walked her to her bedroom where she crawled under the covers fully clothed. He shut her door, returning to the kitchen to finish the pies.

With the pies in the oven, Jeff checked on the rest of the meal. The turkey was already thawing in the refrigerator. He removed one of the legs and threw it in a soup pot with chopped onion, celery, carrot, salt, pepper, and water, bringing the mixture to a simmer. He popped on the lid, pulled the pies out to cool and tidied up the kitchen. He changed into workout gear and went for a run, the air and open road refreshing after the long car ride.

Jeff ran his boyhood trails, enjoying the old neighborhood but perplexed by his mother's current state. He returned home to shower, then checked on his mother, reassured by her deep snores. Jeff walked into the kitchen, surprised to see his father.

"You're home." His father still wore his overcoat. Jeff hugged the big man. "Where's your mother?"

"She went to bed around three."

"She's been doing that a good bit lately. Don't know what that's all about."

"Feel like soup for dinner? I need to add some rice and it will be ready." He changed the subject, not ready to talk about her yet.

"Thanks for fixing dinner. Soup sounds great on this cold day."

"I followed Mom's recipe, the one you like. I figure something light tonight so we can load-up tomorrow." Jeff tasted the soup. He added salt and a pinch of Indian spice with the rice.

The two men ate in silence, avoiding the topic of mother and wife, the evening news a convenient diversion. Jeff cleared the dishes while his father brought out the scotch. He filled two glasses. Jeff sat on the couch, his father in the big chair by the fire.

"What's going on with Mom?" Jeff asked. Across the room, two disembodied eyes appeared in the lazy-boy chair. They blinked. Jeff choked on his drink, coughing and spitting his scotch back into the glass.

"Are you okay, son? Want some water?"

Jeff waved him off and gave Bill an aggravated look as he recovered. "I'm okay."

"I think she's depressed. She's in bed most nights when I get home. It started after you left last Christmas. She seems to be getting worse lately and I don't know what to do. We don't talk except on the weekends when she's up and I'm home."

"She told me she wanted to be a grandmother."

"That's part of it. I think your divorce last year affected your mother more than we knew."

"It was hard for me, too. It took a lot of work to get over Martine. I've been in counseling since last winter. It sounds like Mom needs counseling, too. If you want, I can try to find someone for her. I think she's depressed. She needs to talk with someone and work through the pain."

"I don't understand why she's depressed. She has everything here, her family, her friends, and our home. I know I work a lot and she's alone much of the time. I'd hoped that your being home would help."

"It doesn't work like that. The pain is in her heart or her head and you and I don't have any say how it affects her. Only a doctor can help her pull it to the surface. Sometimes it takes medication. I'll find someone for her to see but you'll have to get her to go and this will take time. You should be with her to talk to the doctor and understand so you can help her."

"I don't know if I can the take time off now, Jeff. There's so much going on at the plant that we need to finish so everyone can leave for the holidays. I've never been one to go to doctors or hospitals. Your mother did all those things." He sighed.

"It's okay. We'll do it together. I'm here this weekend and maybe we can find a doctor. We can get an appointment while I'm home during the Christmas. The three of us can go and it won't be so hard for you after I go back in January. You know, it's funny." Jeff swirled his drink. "I never thought you and I were very much alike, but we are in many ways. We both feel compelled to finish once we've started something. It's like that when I race. It was like that with Martine, too. I just couldn't accept that our marriage was over and it nearly killed me."

"I'm sorry. I didn't know how hard that time was for you. I wished we talked sooner. You've done well, son."

"Thanks, Dad, I'm going to be fine, but it appears depression runs in our family. I have it, and Mom has it. Therapy has helped me. It can help her. I had a friend who wasn't so lucky."

"Okay, we will all go to therapy. I'm glad you're home. Thanksgiving wouldn't be the same without you."

"I wish I could stay after, but I have to go back and finish exams. I'll be back next week for the Marathon. I get in late so I'm going to stay downtown on Friday night. It will be easier to focus on the race and to get up and run the next morning. I'll come home after the race."

"Don't you want to stay here?"

"It will be easier for me to be downtown. I have to meet my manager, and there might be other obligations." Jeff checked on the disembodied eyes that still floated above the chair. "Do you want to watch me race? The course passes nearby at the reservoir. You could see me at the halfway point then drive down to the stadium for the finish."

"I'd love to watch you run." He stood. "I better go check on your mother and I think I'll go to bed, too. Thank you for dinner and for coming home. We've missed you, goodnight."

"Goodnight, Dad." Jeff swirled what remained of his drink and ice.

"Well, that was quite the eventful day," Bill spoke for the first time, the voice came from the area around the eyes. "I forgot the complications of family life. I'm glad to hear you will stay downtown the night before the race. You're a smart lad to not stay here with your mother in such a state."

"It was quite the day." Jeff poured a second scotch. "I'd offer you one, but you don't look like you're in drinking shape tonight." Jeff chuckled at the quip. "And don't criticize my mother. As I recall from the bar down at the harbor, you liked to tie one on once upon a time. Your comments aren't helpful." Bill's eyes seemed to flutter like a poor TV signal.

"You love your father, don't you Jeff?"

"I do love him very much. You know, all this time I've thought the conflict was between my father and me. It turns out he's proud of me." He drained the scotch.

"There's nothing like a fathers love. My dad took me to my first marathon. He was so proud of me and my running. He borrowed a sedan from a neighbor and we drove to Laurel where the race started. Mother had given me pancakes with jelly and a thermos of tea for the drive. I was so excited and ready to race hard but my coach told me to go out at jogging pace for the first ten miles. I ran with Whitey Michelson, the former world record holder and the great, Clarence DeMar. I had his comic book from the Paris games where he won bronze. I think he was irritated with me, just a boy from the local club tagging to his heals. They'd stop for water and so would I. Eventually they pulled away but I was able to keep up for the most part. Towards the end, the tiredness set in. I'll never forget coming to the city plaza and hearing the crowd roar, my family at the finish line, Mom and Dad so excited. I won a big silver cup that day and a whole chicken for dinner. Dad was so proud." He stopped.

"I'm tired, Bill. The drive and drama wore me out. Tomorrow's going to be a big day, and my mother will need help. I'm going to bed. See you tomorrow."

Bill closed his eyes and was gone, only the faded chair and dying coals of the fire were visible. Jeff went to bed, happy to be at home. He slept.

****

Jeff rose early to log his miles. He made coffee, then read the paper while he waited for his parents to rise. His father came down first, dressed in khakis and a flannel shirt, ready for the day. Jeff's mom emerged later in her robe and slippers. Her hair needed tending. Jeff tidied a few stray wisps. He placed his arms over her shoulders and planted a kiss on her head.

"I'm sorry I couldn't stay up, honey. I don't know why I've been so tired lately." Her eyes were bloodshot.

Jeff patted her gently on the back and poured her coffee. "I finished the pies and the turkey is thawed. I also started on the stuffing. Is 2 or 3-o'clock good for dinner?"

"If that's what you boys want. I'll get started on the sides if you'll take care of the turkey. I've always hated those big, smelly birds."

The day was uneventful, the home filled with smells of the holiday: cinnamon, sage, onion, and roasted turkey. The three ate in the formal dining room, the cloth napkins and good china out for the occasion. Jeff told them about school and his upcoming race. His mother sipped white wine, the Seagram's bottle back in the cupboard. After they cleared the dishes, the men retired to the living room for football and naps. Jeff's father nodded

144

in his chair, Jeff reclined on the couch and Bill claimed the Lazy-boy once again. Jeff could see his faded shape, apparently napping as well.

****

Jeff stopped at the base of Satyr Hill. He smelled the ozone before he saw Bill, leaning against a split rail fence.

"You're back. I can see you today."

"There is a lot of pain in that house. It brought me back."

"Don't go haunting or linking or whatever it is you do to my parents. They have enough going on without a ghost."

"I won't haunt them. It's you and me for better or worse. We're like an old married couple." Bill chuckled.

Jeff ignored the joke. "Let's get on with this workout."

"You're good and warmed up, so I want you to run to the top at three-quarters race speed. Work into it. The last portion will be steep and I don't want you to strain. If you need to, back off the pace. I want you to run one repetition up to the top to get used to the grade. Jog back here when you've finished." Jeff set off, eager for the test.

The start of the hill was mild, the first mile brisk but easy after the rest days following the cross-country race. He felt excited about the challenge and the summit. Jeff pushed up the slight grade and the second mile before the road made a turn and took a steeper slope, the familiar fatigue building. It took additional effort to maintain pace and form. The road made a final turn, the new incline drastic for the climb to the top. Jeff labored, his leg muscles fatigued and leaden. He struggled to the crest over the last 100-meters with short steps, his breaths strained.

Jeff crossed the top of the hill and jogged in place. Towson's businesses and college lay before him, hiding the remainder of the course. He stretched a little then ran slowly down to the base where Bill waited.

"What did you think, lad?"

"She's a bitch. That last portion is murder."

"Exactly. That's where I made my move. The other runners couldn't stay with me when I pushed through the top. They all fell back and that's our strategy too. I want you to leave it all there on that hill."

Jeff nodded, conscious of the queasy feeling of lactic acid that coursed through his circulatory system. What would the hill feel like after fifteen-miles at 5:20 pace? He shook the thought off. "Well, I guess we're ready. I have to head back to school tomorrow. Are you ready to head back?"

"Go ahead and return to school. Finish what you need to finish and I'll wait for you here. I'm staying in Baltimore. I'm home." Bills face softened.

"Where will you stay?" He walked back to the pale, shade of a man. "You're not staying with my parents, are you?"

"No, I have a place I can stay if you'll take me there tonight."

CHAPTER 17

Jeff drove to the Harbor. He hadn't been down to the Point since high school when he and his friends would sneak into the bars. The cobblestones of Thames Street rumbled under the car tires. He parked and walked to the old pub. Bill walked beside him up the steps. They stopped outside of the bright blue door of The Black Cat Pub, the hissing black feline on the sign hung above the door.

"Shall we?" Jeff asked and opened the heavy wood door. The bar was dim and smelled of stale beer.

"Go to the last booth in the back," Bill pointed.

Jeff sat down across from Bill. The wood was sticky and intricately carved with graffiti, initials, and dates from over the years. The old barmaid walked up, her shoulders hunched, she was bent at the waist with one hand attached to her hip. She wore a pale shade of pink lipstick, and heavy eyeshadow, her beehive hairdo disheveled. Jeff guessed her to be in her late 60's with a few lumps where curves might have once been.

"What're you sittin' back here for?" She asked abruptly.

"Do you mind? I like the back booth."

"People say it's haunted. I've never seen anything, but others have seen things. Lights flicker or things move." She stood with her pad ready to take his order. "Do you want anything? My feet are killing me."

"Just a beer. Natty's fine." Mr. Boh smiled appreciatively from the neon sign on the opposite wall. The old woman shuffled off.

"That's Betty. Time and mopping-up behind the bar haven't been too kind to the girl. She was a real beauty once." Bill sighed. "You've wondered why I am so protective of you with your female attachments. Betty was mine. She changed everything and she was why I did what I did." Bill paused, following the barmaid as she brought Jeff's beer.

"Here you go, honey. You can move to the bar if that old ghost shows up."

Jeff smiled at Bill. "I'm sure I'll be okay here, but thanks."

Bill nodded. "That's my cup, there in front of the mirror behind the bar. My name is etched on the back. I won the race you're going to run in 1930. It was one of my last races. I gave the cup and a picture of me winning to the proprietor. He gave me beers. I liked coming here. Betty was small then, just a child when I raced. We became reacquainted when I was working at the point and she worked here for her father."

"She was nice to me and listened when I needed someone to talk to, usually in the back seat of my car. I didn't mean for it to happen, and then she was pregnant. It was always a struggle or tense at home back then. Betty wanted me to support her and get her out of the bar. Life became torture, torn between two women. I couldn't handle the stress."

"Is this the bar I saw in your dream?"

"It is."

"What about the priest. He seemed nice, and he looked out for you."

"No, even he let me down. He said I had to face my troubles and wouldn't hear my confession or give me absolution until I fixed things between Charlene and Betty. There wasn't any fixing and I could only see one way out."

"The car? You took your life in the car?"

"Yes. That way, at least Charlene got my union benefits. But then I never knew my child. She'd be thirty-something now, a bit older than you."

"But you've been here and they know about the ghost?"

"I haven't been back since she was really little. All the floating around I told you about. It feels good to be back. I used to blink the lights and move salt shakers for fun." He grinned as the salt shaker moved to Jeff's hand.

"You can't scare me anymore Bill. I'd like to see the cup. That's really cool."

"There should be a picture of me crossing the finish line too. I'm getting weak, so I'm going to go. Meet me here next week, the night before the race."

Jeff nodded as the ghost faded. Betty walked up.

"Want another?"

"No, I need to get home. Can I ask you about that silver cup behind the bar?"

She turned to look. "What about it? We use it to collect bottle caps. Just an old piece of junk someone gave my father once. It has no significance. Take a look if you want. It's been here as long as I have."

Jeff paid his tab, pulled on his coat and walked to the bar. The cup was large, ornate, and beautiful, just as he had seen it in the dream at Ziggy's. The picture was partially covered by a banner for Cinco de Mayo and a good build up of dust.

****

Jeff said goodbye to his mother, having hugged his father goodbye earlier that morning. "Promise me you will set an appointment, Mom. Depression isn't a good thing to let hang around. I know."

"I should be stronger, but sometimes I feel frozen. It's difficult to do anything and I don't want to get up. You give me hope."

"It's not about strength, Mom. It's about getting better and talking about how you feel, like we are now. There's no judgment. Go see the doctor. Dad's going to go with you, so you'll have him and you can always call me. I'll be back next weekend, then for Christmas, so we'll have lots of time together." He kissed her goodbye and walked to his car for the drive back to campus.

Libby popped into his thoughts while driving down the lonesome highway, noting the barren trees and fields. The year before, it had been Martine consuming his thoughts as he drove. The overpass that had been so appealing appeared ahead. Jeff pulled over to the emergency strip. The bridge column that once called like a siren was only a lonely column. It held no attraction now. His tire tread, a swerving fishtail, still marked the pavement. The overpass faded from view in his rearview mirror, another ghost fading.

Bill had helped him get in shape. He'd also brought him back to help his mother and understand his father. He'd keep his agreement with the old ghost and help him find peace, though unsure how he'd achieve that goal. Maybe he'd just disappear, like the overpass.

****

Jeff stood in front of the class at the professor's lectern. The room was dark except for the projector and screen. He wore his only suit with the black and gold striped tie Libby bought him last summer. He couldn't see the faces of his classmates in the bright light and wondered if she might be watching. His group presented last.

"Good afternoon," he began. "We're excited to introduce a new product, Tan-d-Wipes. Each of you is receiving a sample of the combination sunscreen and moisturizing wipe." His partners passed samples down the aisles of the repurposed barbecue wipes, marked-up with the Tan-d-wipe logo on one side and a cartoon character's face on the other. "I'll begin with an overview to highlight the product, placement, price, and promotion for this unique sunscreen product."

"The tanning lotion and sunscreen market is crowded. The first slide illustrates how a typical grocery or drug store shelf might look with various bottles and tubes. There is little differentiation between containers, lotion strength, or price. Our product changes that. There's no bulky bottle or greasy lotion. The sunscreen wipes on clean and each one will cover a face, back, or arm in one wipe." Jeff's partner demonstrated on her arms and then tossed the wipe into a trash bin with a flourish. "You wipe and toss. It won't leak in your purse, pocket, or beach bag. It also takes up little space on the shelf or in a drawer."

"The Tan-d-Wipe is a unique product." Jeff held up a box, with the same red and white striped pattern as the sample his partner had passed out. "Here is a mock-up of a twelve-pack, designed to cover Mom, Dad, and little Wesley's face and arms at the soccer match. The placement stands out on the shelf." The slide showed the box amidst the various colored and shaped bottles. "It looks like a box of candy, and that's deliberate. We want the product to be both an intentional purchase and an impulse buy, attractive to children and adults."

"Pricing is low. We'll go over the proforma in a moment, but because we don't have to buy or produce bottles, the cost is relatively low per unit. That leaves promotion, which will also be fairly inexpensive. We would start with print advertising because that's the domain our spokesman occupies.

"Let me introduce our spokesman, professional sun tan champion, Zonker Harris from *Doonesbury*." Jeff's teammates slid forward a life-size cutout of the cartoon character in his beach trunks, sandals, and tank top, stopping next to Jeff at the podium. Zonker held a large mock-up wipe with the caption, "This baby won me the George Hamilton Cocoa-Butter Open." The class cheered.

****

Jeff gathered his slides, exhilarated and a little damp under the arms from the presentation. One of his group members came up. "We're headed to Ziggy's. You coming, Jeff?"

"I'll see you there. A cold beer sounds great right now."

"See you there and bring Zonk."

Jeff pulled on his backpack and tucked the cut-out under his arm. He walked up the steps to the back of the room where Dr. Mason waited.

"Last time, I was the one walking out, Mr. Dillon. Good job today. I'm proud to have a presentation of that caliber in my class."

"Thank you. I'm glad things worked out. You've taught me a lot."

"I want to introduce you to Robert Flynn. He took my class some years ago and is always kind enough to come back and help me grade the projects. Robert, have you met Jeff?"

"I've seen you race. I run the occasional 10k, but not at your level."

"It's a lot of work but I love it. I can't do it forever."

"Jeff, was this your creative idea?"

"I can only take partial credit. You know, Matt, your old fraternity brother?"

"Sure, I know Matt. Watch the word old, okay? How's he doing?"

"He's great. We were eating barbecue at Simoes and he was reading *Doonesbury* and laughing about Zonker. I was wiping the grease off my fingers with their wipes. One thing led to another and it all came together there."

"Jeff, you didn't know, but the product you presented is similar to one we're working on at the agency. We like fresh ideas, which is why we help Dr. Mason with this class. We've gotten a few from the program over the years. I'd like you to pitch the Tan-d-Wipe idea to my creative team. Work with them this next semester as an intern if it suits you. If you like our firm, there may be a position when you graduate. What do you say?"

"Yes, of course. I'd love that opportunity. Thank you, Mr. Flynn."

"Call me Bob. You can start after the Christmas break. Bring your friend, Zonker with you. He's a popular guy."

"Thank you, Bob. I will." He stood with Dr. Mason while Flynn walked out.

"Well done, Jeff. I'd love to see another graduate working at the agency." The two shook hands. "Now I am headed home and I believe your team is waiting for you at an establishment called Ziggy's. I won't hold you up any longer. Goodnight."

Jeff stood in the darkened room, savoring a feeling he'd only occasionally felt crossing the finish line.

CHAPTER 18

December

Jeff tapped his toe impatiently, ready to finish his session with Dr. Black, the last item on his to-do list. An easy talk with the good doctor, a quick trip to the airport and then a racing weekend. He lived for those days; an air flight, nice hotel, good food and a few beverages with friends, then the race. He was ready. He exhaled, and sat back in the battered armchair.

"How are you today?" Dr. Black asked.

"I'm anxious, but in a good way. I leave for Baltimore tomorrow and race the day after. I'm ready."

"How so? I know you've trained hard this past summer and fall. What will make this performance different than your Olympic Trials race?"

"My training's been more consistent. It's been almost perfect and that's the biggest factor. I've averaged 115-miles per week since mid-June and that alone gives me confidence. But I've also done the hard runs and I'm sharp. I won the cross-country meet recently over two very good collegians. I felt I could have kept going and run the race a second time at the same pace with the same results. The preparation for this marathon has been so different from what I did last spring for the Trials."

"That's great. I wish you luck."

"I'll need it. There are always things you don't count on that can happen. It could be the weather, shoes, or fluid intake. There are any number of things that can interrupt a good effort. A little luck this time would be welcome."

"Will you see your family?"

"I just came back from seeing them over Thanksgiving. It was a good time, but also difficult. My father and I got along well. We had a few nice days together, but my mother is having problems. I think she's depressed. My divorce took a toll on her and I don't know what else. She's drinking a lot, which is something new. My dad and I are going to get her in counseling."

"Counseling can only help. I hope your mother will be okay. I'm curious how you patched things up with your father?"

"I'd built up issues, feeling guilty about pursuing my dream and ashamed my marriage had failed. My father told me he's proud of me for doing my best with school and running. I told him about counseling. I think he understands what I went through last year. He's coming to the race."

"You've made great progress. All those items you listed were major issues that bothered you last summer. You seem to have a good balance now and you're handling your stressors. Let's change focus. Randy, the coach at the university called. He was concerned about you. I told him I'd talk with you. What was his concern?"

"I was hanging out at the track working things out. They were the same things you and I discuss, my training, Martine, school, and Libby. It helps to talk like you and I do. But I guess he saw me talking to myself and that freaked him out."

"That's it? That doesn't sound like much? Are you talking to yourself?"

"Yes, sometimes. I just do what we do here and work through things, pros and cons."

"It probably isn't a good idea to talk out loud, out in the open. People might become concerned. But there's nothing wrong with working issues out."

"Randy thought it was strange for me to be alone in the bleachers, where I meet my coach most days."

"How is that going? I haven't heard you mention him?"

"He's gone home to Baltimore. I won't see him until the race. That will be the end of our working relationship. He's done all he could to help me and I will be on my own again."

"Why aren't you working with him after the race?"

"He's old and tired and told me he wants to stay in Baltimore and rest. I don't need him anymore. Next semester I want to focus on school and my career after graduation. There's and internship I'm going to take."

"That sounds reasonable. Wasn't there something else you couldn't tell me last time?"

"It had to do with my coach. Our relationship has been up and down. I lost Libby along the way. I was anxious about seeing my father at Thanksgiving. Everything has worked out, except Libby. That relationship is probably over. I've heard she may be seeing someone new. It stings a little, but I can accept her choice. I didn't have the time and the energy to pursue her. My coach was right. The race, school, my family are enough right now. Can you write a note to Randy? He took my athletic privileges away and won't let me train at the university until he hears from you. He didn't want me freaking out in front of the team."

"I don't blame him." She smiled. "You seem fine and I think we're finished for now. I'll send Randy a note. Let me know when you get back from Baltimore and you can call me for follow-up if you need to talk during exams. I'm always happy to see you."

Jeff shook the Doctor's hand, relieved. He'd lied to her or at least left out the part about Bill's ghost staying in Baltimore. Hopefully he'd return without Bill, just a normal graduate student who wasn't haunted, a student who raced the marathon.

****

The flight attendant's voice woke him, his engine induced sleep restless with the upcoming race and seeing Bill again. He'd enjoyed the ghost free week. Jeff pushed the thoughts away, knowing he had a very specific job to complete in the next twenty-four hours. It would require his whole focus and effort. Jeff stretched in the narrow coach seat, then sought diversion in the in-flight magazine touting 'Charm City,' the old port makeover dreamed up by the city fathers. The harbor would soon have a new ballpark to complement the aquarium and convention center. They'd carefully blended the old with the new, leaving the tree-lined, cobbled streets of Fell's Point and Little Italy amongst the new buildings and corporate headquarters in the harbor.

"Ladies and gentlemen, please put your seats and trays in their upright position. We will arrive in Baltimore shortly," the attendant announced. Jeff paged through the section on Fells Point, looking for The Black Cat among the quaint restaurants and bars listed. The plane banked slowly, providing a view of the harbor through the circular window. Moments later, the landing gear dropped, and the plane touched down. "Ladies and gentlemen," she greeted the passengers, "welcome to Charm City."

Jeff disembarked with his travel bag in hand. He wore his sponsor's gear and jeans with a heavier, leather jacket for the cold day. He walked briskly to the baggage area, where a man held a sign with his name printed and the marathon logo. They drove downtown quickly, the traffic thin on a Friday afternoon.

"You running tomorrow?" the driver asked.

"I am. Do you know what the temperature will be in the morning?"

"Dunno, but it'll be cold. I don't get it. You fellas run a long way. The telethon is twenty-five miles if I'm not mistaken. Horses don't run that far. I like the ponies, one lap around the track. Twenty-five miles is a long, freaking way." He whistled.

"The marathon," Jeff corrected him gently, "is 26.2-miles, and it is a long way. I've trained for it though, so hopefully the race will go by quickly. It will take close to two and a half hours."

"You gonna win?"

"I've got a shot."

"How much money you gonna get for winnin'?"

"Not as much as you can make with the ponies, but not a bad day's work either. If I place, it might be a couple hundred bucks. Winner will get one-thousand. It's not bad. The big races pay more, five figures."

"I'm no math genius, but that's not much per mile." The driver shook his head, and Jeff grinned, nodding in agreement.

The van pulled into the downtown Sheraton that served as race headquarters. Jeff wished the driver luck at the racetrack and gave him a five-dollar bill.

He checked-in at the front desk where a message awaited from his manager, Ken.

Jeff, I won't be able to make the race this weekend. Have a good run and call me after with the results. No worries. I've enclosed a copy of your contract for the coming year. I'll send a check when I receive the signed copy. You'll find a bag with gear and shoes in your room. Enjoy & good luck, Ken

Jeff folded the note, relieved to have one less worry, his contract with Converse secure for the year. He walked across the lobby to the registration table to pick up his credentials. A man with thinning hair and wire-rimmed glasses stopped him.

"Jeff Dillon?"

"Yes."

"I'm Sean McIntyre, from the *Sun*. Do you have a few minutes? I'd like to interview you for the race edition tomorrow."

"Sure." The two found a quiet spot in the lounge, warmed by the sun that poured through the large lobby windows.

"You're from Maryland?"

"That's right."

"I thought I remembered you from high school. Your team finished second at states a few years back. What have you been doing?"

"I'm in graduate school down in North Carolina, running for Converse. I've been racing on the roads and ran in the Olympic Trials Marathon last spring. It's great to be back racing in Maryland."

"Your bib number eight, but your 2:18 seeds you number five. How do you feel about your chances?"

"I'm ready. I put in a good seven months training with this race my sole focus. I practiced on Satyr Hill last week. Who else is running?"

"Wilson's the favorite with a 2:12. I'm interviewing him later. I want to hear what it was like to lead the Trials last summer. Then there's Ron Hill, our lone Olympian. He has the fastest time on paper at 2:09, but the Englishman's getting up in age. I don't see him up front at the end of the race. You'd know the others, mostly local, Schaffer, Goodman, Robinson, and Smith, all 2:21 or faster. You ran against Schaffer in high school, didn't you?"

"Yes, I did. Schaffer's good. He finished just in front of me at the Trials. Neither of us ran very well that day. Hopefully, tomorrow will be a better day for both of us."

"My picks for tomorrow are Wilson, Schaffer, and you, in that order."

"Great, you have me on the podium. Can I ask you a question? Have you ever heard of a runner from the thirties named, Bill Atlee?"

"Sure, he's a legend. Old Bill won this race several times in the early days. There's a big file on him at the paper. He was a newspaper delivery boy at the *Sun* and has a lot of records in the mid-Atlantic. I believe he ran at the Amsterdam Games. Why do you ask?"

"I came across him in a magazine for the Hall of Fame. Shame how he died."

"It was suicide. Bill had retired by then and worked at the steel mill. Oh, pardon me, but I see Ron Hill across the lobby and I need to interview him while he's downstairs. Good luck tomorrow. I have a feeling I'll be interviewing you after the race."

McIntyre jogged over to the small crowd that moved through the lobby. Jeff marveled at the diminutive Englishman with the droopy mustache. He looked as fit as he had at Munich, twelve years before, leading the Olympians out of the stadium to the city beyond on Jeff's TV screen.

CHAPTER 19

Jeff jogged a few city blocks to get the kinks out, stretching near the harbor. The icy water didn't seem to affect the gulls that screeched and bobbed on the ripples. He jogged back to the hotel, showered and napped the rest of the afternoon.

Rising after sunset, Jeff dressed for the frigid night. After a short taxi drive, he arrived on Thames Street. The contrast from the modern downtown skyscrapers overlooking the harbor to the quaint village only blocks away was amazing. He walked back in time through the harbor fog and cobbled street. Boats swayed in the dark water; their mast lights rippled in the mist.

"Not much different than in Bill's day." Jeff spoke out loud, enjoying the brisk air and harbor sounds. He stood at a cross street, an old stone church on one side, the Black Cat on the opposite corner in a row of bars and tourist shops. Bill approached, his coat flowing and hat low.

"I have one request before we head across the street for your dinner. Would you take me inside?" Bill motioned towards the church.

"Bill, I only want to eat and rest. I need to focus on the race. I don't feel like going with you to church. Anyway, I'm sure it's locked up for the night."

"I think you'll find the side door open. I can go in if you take me." Bill walked up the path and beckoned to Jeff. "Trust me and take me in, I think it's part of the plan. Please, it won't take long."

"What the hell, Bill. I can't believe I'm even thinking of doing this." Jeff walked to the door shaking his head and hoping the door was locked. The door swung open easily and shut behind with a clang. Inside, the church was shadowy, illuminated only by a few lamps and votive candles in the alcoves.

"Young man," a fat, old priest walked quickly down the aisle towards Jeff. He reached them out-of-breath. "I'm just locking up before the bar crowd hits the street. They wander in and it can be a bit messy in the morning for Mass. Would you like to come back tomorrow?"

"I won't be long, Father. I want to say a prayer for a friend." Jeff glanced at Bill. He nodded.

"Call me Monsignor. I can't say no to a request like that." He bowed slightly.

Bill whispered to Jeff. "My old priest. After all these years. The old boy hasn't missed many meals." Bill chuckled, but his demeanor quickly changed. "I needed him to take my confession. I had nowhere to turn and no one to talk to."

"My friend committed suicide many years ago. Can he be blessed and forgiven?"

"We are encouraged to intercede for the dead, to pray for their souls. That was your first question. The second question is more complicated. Taking a life, especially one's own is the gravest of sins. Are you okay, my son? Is there something more that bothers you? Have you had thoughts about suicide?" The priest waited for Jeff to respond.

"I have in the past, but I'm better now. I'm here to run the marathon tomorrow and I'm having dinner next door at the Black Cat. I thought I'd pray for the man that helped me get here. You might remember him, Bill Atlee, an Olympian from the 30's."

"I remember him well. He was a troubled soul and loved the Black Cat. He loved it a bit too much I'm afraid. But how do you know about Bill? That was a long time ago."

"I became a fan when I decided to run the race. I've researched him and was motivated by his story. As I trained, I learned about him. We share some history, so here I am, ready to race tomorrow. This is the end of my journey with him."

"It's funny you mention the Black Cat. I believe the woman he was involved with and her daughter still work there. It was the family business." The priest had Bill's attention. "It's kind of you to pray for him. If I had taken your kindness and used it with Bill, we might still have him around." Bill stopped pacing and returned to the conversation. "But I was a young priest, and I insisted he work out his problems on his own. He was married to one woman and they had children. He became involved with another from the bar and she got pregnant. He came to me for absolution for his sins. I wouldn't give it to him even though he confessed. We didn't understand mental illness very well back then. We should have talked more and I should have counseled him to help him with his guilt. After he took his life, I felt terrible. I've prayed for him every day since. I've had a hard time forgiving myself." The old priest sighed.

"Tell him I don't blame him." Bill leaned in behind Jeff.

"Monsignor, I'm sure he doesn't hold you responsible. He took action, not you. Maybe we can say a prayer of peace and ask forgiveness for all of us. It would do me good." The Monsignor put his hand on Jeff's shoulder and Bill placed his on top of the priests.

"My, I just had the biggest chill." He shook his hand. "Let us pray. In the name of the Father, Son, and Holy Spirit." All three made the sign of the cross. "Heavenly Father, we come before you to pray for our brother, Bill, and to pray for his soul. We ask for his and our own forgiveness, before you, your son Jesus, and the Blessed Virgin." The prayer was short. Bill and the priest crossed themselves again as they walked toward the door, stopping at the alcove devoted to Mary.

"Can I light a candle and say one more prayer, Monsignor?" The old priest nodded while Jeff and Bill knelt, side by side, reciting the Hail Mary. He stood to light a candle. "I remember that one from high school with my friends."

Jeff followed the priest and Bill followed Jeff. Bill whispered. "Will you look at us, the father, son, and not-so-holy ghost." Bill laughed. Jeff rolled his eyes.

"Thank you, Monsignor. I'm sure Bill is grateful for the prayers."

"It does me good to know others care about the man, that he wasn't forgotten. You're a good boy, but you're not Catholic, are you?"

"No, I'm not."

"If you come back, I would be glad to teach you about the church. It's nice to meet someone with your empathy. There's hope for this generation."

"I just might take you up on that offer, Monsignor. I know there's more to life than running and I've experienced grace. I'll try to come back and see you when I'm home. I'm Jeff." The two men shook hands before the man and ghost stepped out the door.

Bill let out a deep breath outside. The ozone smell was noticeable and he had changed. Standing before Jeff was the well built, middle-aged steel-worker in coveralls. He had dark black hair and bright brown eyes. It was the man who'd taken his life fifty years before. "Let's go see my daughter."

Jeff felt a chill walking slowly up the brick hurricane steps with Bill close behind. Turning the doorknob, he stepped in, greeted by the blue Colts banners hanging from the ceiling. He hadn't noticed them on the first visit. The team had left Baltimore for Indianapolis the previous spring in the middle of the night, leaving the city and fans in an uproar. Thank God something was of his own era. He paused at the long, polished bar and the trophy from Bill's past. Bill breezed past him and took his normal seat in the back. Jeff sat down across from him.

"What can I get you?"

The waitress's appearance startled Jeff. She was tall with short, spiked, platinum blond hair and dark eyebrows. Her brown eyes sparkled like Bill's.

"Oh, a beer would be great, and a menu."

"Natty Boh OK?"

Jeff nodded, noticing a tattoo on her thigh just below the hem of her shorts that spelled Charm City in old script.

"Working for the Chamber of Commerce?" He joked.

She followed his gaze. "Oh, yeah, it seemed like a fun thing at the time so we all did it a few years back. Everyone down here at the point appreciates the 'Charm City' campaign and tourism. But Baltimore isn't just crab cakes, Mr. Boh, and the Utz girl. We all got these tattoo's showing the real Baltimore." She hiked her hem further up her thigh to reveal a second tattoo of a grinning rat with sharp teeth, perched over the words. They both laughed as she skipped off to get the beer and menu.

Jeff removed his jacket and pushed his sweatshirt sleeves up. Bill's ice-cold hand clamped Jeff's bare arm. "She's not for you, Jeffrey"

The touch froze his wrist, the pain shooting up his arm like electric current. Ozone poured across the table choking him.

Jeff pulled his arm free with a jerk, then sank heavily into the corner of the booth. His wrist burned from the icy grip. The girl sat the beer down and told Jeff she'd be right back for his order.

Bill spoke first. "Leave my daughter alone, Jeffrey, she's not for you. You don't need to be fooling around with a woman before your race. We have work to finish."

"Geeze, Bill. I was joking with her and she was just doing her job. I don't have to be here with you. I could have been back to the pasta feed at the hotel instead of this. It was your idea to come here, remember? And we just went to church. What gives with you?"

"Please calm down. I'm sorry if that hurt, I'm a little high strung tonight. We're so close to completing what we set out to do and then seeing her." He followed the girl with his eyes. "She looks just like her mother back in the day. She's lovely."

The girl approached. "Whew." She fanned her face. "Sewer gas is bad back here. Do you want to move?"

"No, I'll just order." He checked his watch. The pasta feed would be over by the time he caught a cab back to the hotel, and he hadn't eaten since that morning. He needed calories for the next day and found himself ravenous.

"I'll have the crab cakes and a double order of Old Bay fries." She left them after taking the order.

"What the hell, Bill. I have to conserve my energy and you're siphoning it out of me. I get it about being excited about seeing her, but I'm not going to go off with her tonight. I'm just trying to be friendly."

"I'm sorry, son. You have nothing to fear from me. That won't happen again, I promise." Both were quiet. Jeff rubbed his frozen wrist.

With nothing to say to the old ghost, Jeff focused on the cup across the room. The girl was busy with other customers, going in and out of the kitchen and pouring beers at the tap. She came back with his order. The smells of Old Bay, crab, and hot oil were restorative. Jeff covered the fries with vinegar and a good glug of ketchup on the side. He dug in, the food moved quickly off the plate, a second beer on the way.

"You know you're in a haunted booth," the waitress brought his beer.

"So I've heard. The older waitress told me that last week. "

"Oh, you met my mother. I hope she was nice. She gets cranky, especially when she works late to close up for me. She ran the bar for a long time, and now it's mine. It's been in our family for a long time."

"Do you believe in ghosts?"

"No, I don't. I believe in what I can see and touch." She knocked on the graffitied table. "I'm studying psychology in college. I believe in science. Once I get my degree and a real job, I hope to sell this place. How about you? Are you visiting?"

"I'm in graduate school, though Baltimore was once my home. I'm back to run the marathon tomorrow."

"That's great. Good luck. I've always enjoyed sports. Supposedly, my father was quite the runner. That's him." She pointed to a small picture above the cup. "I never knew my father and my mother won't talk about him. He died before I was born. Enjoy your meal and welcome back to Baltimore. I need to go take care of the other customers." She left abruptly.

"She doesn't know anything about me. A shame," Bill sighed.

Jeff finished his meal and beer. He got up and went to the bar across from the cup with Bill close behind. "I'll settle up," he told the girl. "I know a little bit about the man, if your interested." Jeff nodded at the picture as she worked the tap. She delivered the beers to other guests, then came back and ran up Jeff's ticket.

"I read about him in a running magazine and since I was coming back to Baltimore to race, I did a little research. He was an Olympian. It turns out that he and I had a lot in common. He won the race I'm running tomorrow, back in 1930. You can look him up at the Pratt library. He won hundreds of races and was known as the Baltimore Sun Paperboy." Bill stood directly behind him.

"That's nice to know someone besides me cares about him. No one should be forgotten. He looks happy in the photo. I wish I knew him when I was growing up."

"Tell her I would have loved to know her too." Bill joined the conversation.

"I'm sure he feels the same way about you. I have to go and get ready for tomorrow. Dinner was perfect. Thank you."

"Good luck tomorrow. I hope you win like my dad. Stop in anytime." She took the picture down and hugged it to her chest.

Jeff walked out with Bill close behind. They stood under a lamp post. Old Bill was back, his time-worn face graced by a smile. "Thank you, Jeff. That was wonderful to see her and know that she knows who I am. She doesn't hold a grudge. I'm at peace."

"I'm glad you got to meet her. Now, any last words before I head out."

"You know what to do lad. Go out with the leaders, but no faster than 5:10 to 5:15 for the early miles. If the leaders go faster, I want you to hold back. Wait and push the hill, running strong to the finish. You have prepared well and will do fine."

"I better find a cab and get some sleep, Bill."

"Thank you for this night and all you've done for me, Jeffrey. You've kept your part of the agreement. I can't describe what I feel, seeing my daughter and knowing she doesn't think bad of me is a blessing. Being able to go back to church and see my old priest is a second blessing. I thought the reason I needed to come here was to see you race. Now I'm not so sure. I needed to reconcile with my family and the church and none of this would have happened without you. I'm grateful." He began to disappear, mixing with the fog, the faint smell of his passage mixed with the harbor water.

"Will I see you tomorrow?"

"You will," a voice said from the mist.

Jeff hailed a cab, ready to call it a night and to leave all thoughts of ghosts on the cobbled street.

****

A perfect silhouette lay on his bed, Jeff's shirt with the number pinned to the front, shorts, and racing flats. He folded his warm-up gear and placed it to one side. It was a ritual he'd performed a hundred times over the years on a different bed in a different city. Seeing his gear laid out and ready provided a small comfort. He relaxed despite the monumental task the next morning. He called the front desk for a wake-up call then crawled into bed next to his kit. He slept soundly, uninterrupted by dreams.

CHAPTER 20

The phone rang twice. Jeff sat and stretched, letting the call go unanswered. He turned on the TV news for the weather report, the morning temperature 29-degrees with no wind, the day would be clear and sunny. The marathon God had smiled.

"Perfect." Jeff dressed and pulled on his shoes without socks. Despite the frosty temperatures, he preferred cold toes to potential hot spots. He fixed a cup of coffee from the minibar, packed his bag and was out the door.

The athlete's courtesy room had breakfast laid out. Jeff chose toast with butter, honey and a second cup of coffee. He made a final trip to the bathroom, much nicer and warmer than the port-o-potties at the stadium.

A hotel van transported the athletes to the stadium. The runners were bundled and silent in their concentration. The radio said the temperature had risen to 32-degrees. By race time, it should be mid-thirties. He disembarked, checked-in and went for a jog around the massive brick stadium that sat on a small hill above downtown. Jeff circled the structure, warm from his efforts. He stripped off his sweats. Final decisions included gloves or no gloves, hat or no hat, tee-shirt or no tee-shirt? He could easily toss anything he didn't need during the race, but he wanted his gear perfect. A huge sun emerged over the harbor. It would be warmer later. He dispensed with gloves, hat, and tee-shirt, all shoved back into his bag.

Jeff walked to the start. Schaffer and Wilson were there, along with Smith from George Mason. Robinson and Goodman, the two best locals, jogged up. They took their places up front, while a thousand other runners packed in behind to fill a full city block. Ron Hill squeezed in next to Jeff. He nodded, "Mate."

"Good luck, Ron." Jeff breathed deeply and summoned as much calmness as he could. He felt a chill, not from the cold but from the icon who stood next to him. He knew it would all change in a few minutes, the manic start and long push for the next two hours.

The runners received their final instruction. "Ladies and gentlemen, it's our great honor to welcome the legend, Ron Hill, Olympian, Commonwealth Games, European, and Boston Marathon Champion." He jogged out ten yards and waved to loud cheers.

A brass band played the star-spangled-banner while Fort McHenry and its famous flag were visible in the harbor below.

"Amazing,' he mouthed. Fresh goosebumps rose from excitement, his heart pounded.

The cannon boomed. Ron Hill led the leaders down 33rd Street. Jeff's group quickly separated from the main pack just past the turn onto the parkway. The cheers and footsteps from the amateurs faded to silence, the only sound the footfalls of his pack and the labored breathing. The leaders turned onto Hillen Road where Wilson took the lead, followed by Jeff and eight to ten others. He ran just behind Schaffer and Goodman. His hunch about the weather was correct. The sun felt warm on his back. A light sweat covering his limbs despite the coolness of the day. Jeff took water at 2-miles and the first aid station. He took a sip to keep the fluids in his body and compensate for the evaporation. The leaders passed Morgan State on Perring Parkway, headed towards Towson and the reservoir. He bided time, comfortable with the five-minute miles. He checked his stride and form to make sure everything was in order; he felt good. The miles passed quickly.

Leaving downtown, the leaders entered the lush forest and meadows of Loch Raven reservoir north of the city. They'd soon pass the halfway mark where pace and attrition would mark the start of the real race. Wilson and another runner had pulled away and were out of sight after sequential sub 5-minute miles on the flat section near the reservoir. Jeff held back, running in the chase pack as Bill had advised. He knew the pace was solid, but he was feeling good, the effort measured. The temperature dropped back into the twenties in the shade along the water. Jeff could see the trademark coat of Bill, just before the aid station ahead. He zipped past the man, surprised to see it wasn't Bill, but his father.

"Great run, son. You look fantastic. Top seven! I'll see you at the finish."

Jeff passed by so quickly, there was only time to nod. He chided himself for not recognizing his father, the two so different in height. He grabbed a cup of water off the table and sipped from the cup before tossing it to the side of the road. The half-marathon marker appeared ahead. The attendant called out 1-hour and 10-minutes, the pace fine. He felt comfortable. Jeff's group of five covered the next two-miles to Satyr Hill quickly. Smith was still at Jeff's side, striding smoothly as they approached the base of the hill. Bill's words rang in his head, "I took 'em all down on that bloody hill."

Jeff started the climb. He leaned a small amount to maintain his pace. Goodman had joined him and Smith, the three just behind Schaffer and another runner. They ran tangent to tangent on the serpentine road, working hard, lifting their bodies weight up the incline. Goodman and Smith dropped a few steps back halfway up. Schaffer, Jeff, and Bremer, the other runner in the trio now chased Wilson and the other breakaway runner, silent, working, sweating. They had covered a mile and one-half of the hill with the steepest section just ahead.

Jeff labored as the pitch increased, his knees beginning to ache and lungs burning in the frosty air. The hill felt steeper than he remembered, but there was nothing else to do. Each stride became slightly shorter than the previous stride as they ate up the asphalt. He knew his companions labored too, all focused on the summit and their misery. He'd leave it all there as Bill told him to do. Beads of sweat ran from his brow stinging his eyes. The crest was near, maybe seventy or eighty yards to go. The end couldn't come soon enough, his legs felt like bags of cement. He struggled, determined, head down, focused only on the next step.

The three emerged into bright sunshine at the top and felt the warmth of the sun again. The large leg muscles relaxed somewhat and his breathing smoothed out as the road flattened. Schaffer led, followed by Bremer, then Jeff. An invisible string pulled the three towards downtown in a single file line, ten yards separating one from the other. They were a study in contrast; Schaffer, shorter and compact ran with efficiency. Bremer ran with his eyes fixed on Schaffer's back, his strides purposeful. Jeff ran tall with a long, powerful stride. The three worked their way back to Perring Parkway and the final straight shot to Memorial Stadium. At 20-miles, the official called out 1-hour and 50-minutes, fast enough, coming off of Satyr. Without warning, Jeff came up on the runner who had taken off with Wilson. He was barely moving forward in a survivor's shuffle. Jeff took water at 22-miles, his last drink before the finish. He grabbed a second cup, just to be sure, gulping what he could. He tossed the paper cup. The three raced toward the finish at close to top-end speed. He had measured the expenditure of energy properly. The pace was fast, but he could maintain all the way to the stadium finish.

Jeff passed the 25-mile mark in 2-hours, 18-minutes. "Damn, I was finishing in Milwaukee." The hill had slowed them, but it didn't matter, he had a little over a mile left and felt great.

Focused on the road ahead, Jeff almost ran into the back of Wilson. His head bowed and his stride short and stiff. He barely moved, causing Jeff to go left and the other two to go right. Despair was evident in his eyes, so close to the finish and no way to reach it on an empty tank. He said a silent thank you to Bill for his advice.

Jeff flew past the 26-mile mark and onto 33rd Street with Schaffer and Bremer. Bill had positioned himself by the marker, waving his hat and jumping up and down like a madman.

"Well done, Jeffrey," he shouted above the clapping and cheers of the crowd. "Keep it up, lad. You've made the podium. Now show me a clean pair of heels and go for the win!"

Jeff flew by, puzzled. He hadn't counted his position. He'd been fifth coming off the hill. His mind cleared, he'd passed Wilson and the other runner and was now in the top three. Elated and with the goal in sight, he launched his final sprint, up on his toes and arms driving him forward.

Schaffer and Bremer were to his left, also in full flight. He focused on the finish line scaffolding, 352-yards up the slight hill. Top three was certain and with any luck he might take the win. He'd made the podium. It was a prize he'd desired for so many miles and so long. He felt the lure of victory.

Schaffer pulled slightly ahead. Jeff responded, pouring everything out in top gear. There was a movement in the crowd to his right. Another runner moved beside him, matching him stride for stride. The boy ran effortlessly, whereas Jeff was full out, straining with each step and drive of the arm. The other runner was fresh, and there was nothing he could do. He'd been caught and could end up fourth and off the podium, the worst position in the entire race. There would be no medal, no glory. His emotions swung in the opposite direction, his father waiting ahead somewhere, disappointment the only reward to hang around his neck.

The boy turned to Jeff. He had a shock of black hair and wore a heavy white jersey and black leather shoes. A 'flying-E' blazed on his chest.

"Can I finish with you, Jeffrey?" Young Bill smiled broadly.

The boy from the picture in the bar, his coach, his mentor, and the ghost who'd been with him since May raced beside him. Gratitude and elation flooded his empty body, pushing him onward. Jeff answered. "Why not. Let's do this together."

The two sprinted toward the finish, man and ghost. Schaffer had inched ahead, pulling Bremer with him, Jeff and Bill a half-step behind. Time and place no longer mattered. The clock showed 2-hours and 23-minutes with a little over 100-meters remaining. Schaffer was fresher, stretching his lead to ten yards, Bremer falling back. Jeff held out his hand. "Together?" He took Bill's hand, the warmth of his own keeping the cold of Bill's touch at bay. He held it high in the ether of the finish.

The finish line changed in front of his eyes. It illuminated, a bright aura even brighter than the afternoon sunlight off the harbor covered the streetscape. The stadium and scaffolding disappeared. Schaffer vanished as he crossed the line, followed by Bremer. They were replaced by bleachers filled with people who cheered. The scene had the color of a faded photograph in grays and sepia. A shadow waved excitedly.

"I can see them, Jeff. I can see them all. They're waiting for me." Tears streamed down Bill's cheeks. He waved with his free hand. Jeff wiped his eyes with a quick brush of his hand, his own tears stinging.

"Let me go, Jeff. I can go now. Let me go."

Jeff let go of Bill's hand and lunged for the line. The light flashed and the scene cleared, the precious oxygen heavy with ozone. He walked a few steps, alone. The painted line and scaffolding returned. He bent over and gripped his knees to catch his breath, his lungs heaved, and exhaustion overtook him. His legs trembled and he felt the cold for the first time that day. An arm grasped him around the middle to stand. Jeff wiped his eyes and stood before his father.

"Where's Bill? The man I finished with, where is he?"

"You finished alone, son. You did great. You finished third. Your sprint was magnificent all the way up the hill to the finish." Jeff shivered, the cold magnified by the shadow cast by the stadium. His father put his arm around Jeff's shoulder and pulled him under his overcoat. The warmth from the big man felt wonderful. Jeff wiped his eyes, overcome with emotion; a podium finish, crossing with Bill, and his father by his side. He took in the moment, joyous and thankful. An overwhelmingly tiredness swept over him. He scanned the crowd. Bill should be there to enjoy the moment. Fourth-place came across the line chased in by Goodman for fifth.

"Can we walk?" The two struggled to the drink table where Schaffer pulled on his sweats. "Congrats, on the win," Jeff offered. "You had wheels coming in that I didn't have. That was a great run on a tough course." The two shook hands.

"You looked like you won the race the way you finished." Schafer did a little jog with his hands up. The two laughed. Jeff and his father went to collect his bag so that he could dress. Jeff then jogged a quick cool down run with Schaffer and high school friends who ran the companion 10-k earlier that day. The warm down was their locker room, comparing notes on the course, joking, and catching up, joyful with their work complete.

"I'm very happy with today's race," he told his father while they waited for the race to complete and the results tallied, and he pulled on his winter jacket, hat, and gloves. "The time is a little slower than I'd hoped, but that hill was tough."

"I'm glad you had a good day. It was a thrilling finish."

"The training I did all summer and fall was designed to prepare me for the second half of the race and to finish with a strong kick, and that's what happened. The last 385-yards felt great. I am so glad you were here."

McIntyre stood nearby, jotting notes to his pad. He gave Jeff a thumb's up and a wink.

"I was only off by one for my top three picks. Congratulations. You ran a great race today."

"Thanks." The sense of accomplishment was tangible, his grin as wide as Bill's when they finished.

"So what made the difference today?"

"It was the hill. The three of us attacked there and didn't look back. My coach and I planned it that way."

Jeff chatted with friends while the results were compiled. He rehydrated with beef bouillon from a tent near the finish. The hot beverage, though untraditional, tasted wonderful on a cold day. He switched to National Bohemian just before the awards.

The announcer called the crowd's attention to the podium. Schaffer was called to the top step and gold medal position to stand before the crowd, then Bremer. Jeff heard his name called followed by his time, 2-hours and 23-minutes and 45-seconds. He stepped onto the third step where his medal was placed around his neck, then handed an envelope, the third-place check. The crowd had shrunk as the cool afternoon waned but still applauded with gusto for the three finishers. It felt just as Bill had said it would. Jeff relished the recognition and applause for that moment. He held up his medal to the crowd with the other two, kissed the bronze disk, and tucked the envelope in his pocket. The three shook hands then stepped off the dais as the women were called. It was too bad Bill was not there to share their accomplishment. He'd have enjoyed the moment. Jeff searched the crowd one last time for the raincoat and hat. "Oh, well," Jeff stepped into the crowd to collect his beer and accept the congratulatory handshakes and pats-on-the-back from the other runners. He tipped his cup towards the finish line.

"Thanks, Bill. I couldn't have done this without you." He drained the last sip. Jeff's muscles complained as he walked with his father to the car. The coldness of the day began to settle in. "Can we go somewhere and warm-up before we go home, Dad?

"Anywhere you'd like, son."

"There's a little place down in Fells Point. A friend of mine might be there and I want to thank him and say goodbye. Then we can go see Mom."

CHAPTER 21

The two walked up the steps to the big blue door, cheery and welcoming in the bright, afternoon sun. Jeff spotted the back booth as he entered, empty and holding no interest for him.

"Do you mind sitting at the bar, Dad?" They sat across from the cup. Bill's daughter came out of the kitchen wearing a Colts hoodie, shorts, and sneakers. Her Charm City tattoo peaked from beneath her shorts.

"You came back. How'd the race go?"

"Great, I finished third and made the podium. It was a good day." He jingled the medal that still hung around his neck.

"Congratulations."

"Nice hoodie. Are you pulling for the not-so-home team?"

"You mean the Colt's?" She pinched the logo so it stood out. "Bastards, left in the middle of the night, but old habits die hard. We have our regulars who'll want to watch the game. What will you guys have, a couple of Natty Boh's?"

"I'd like something a little more substantial on a cold day. How does a Guinness sound, Dad?"

"That sounds good."

"Do you all want lunch? The cook just made linguine and clams, best at the Point."

His father nodded affirmatively. "I'm going to wash up. I'll be back in a moment."

"That sounds perfect. We'll take two with garlic bread." Jeff slouched onto a stool, relaxing in the warmth of the pub.

The barmaid started to pour the pints then went into the kitchen to place the order. Jeff took off his medal and weighed the palm-size, bronze medallion. The checkerboard state colors, black, yellow, red, and white decorated one side. The other side featured an outline of the city, etched with the race logo. It had a long red, white and blue ribbon. Jeff leaned over the bar as far as he could and tossed it into the silver cup. The medal landed with a clang that sent bottle caps flying, the ribbon hanging over the side.

Bill's daughter came back with the beers, the light brown foam thick and full. She pulled the medal out by the ribbon, kicking a few of the bottle caps out of the way. "Don't you want this? You worked so hard."

"Your father helped me prepare for the race today. I wouldn't have done so well and won it without him. I'd like it to stay next to his medal. "

She laid the medal down in the cup next to Bill's yellowed one and picked up the small framed picture. "I talked to my mother last night and she told me how their story ended. It's sad but it doesn't change how I feel. I would have liked to know him. I'm Ellie, by the way." They shook hands. She paused, thinking for a moment. "How could my father have helped you?"

"I ran a lot of miles to prepare. When you run for two or three hours at a time, there is a lot to think about. I studied his training and races, and call me crazy, but it started to seem like he was there, an older version of the boy in the picture. I needed a coach after the Olympic Trials last May. I had a bad day and finished last. It turns out it was the same time as his when he won the Trials here in 1928. I was hurt and depressed after the race. Other things were going on in my life that were bothering me. I guess we had a lot in common and I felt like I knew him."

Jeff paused, trying to decide if he should continue. "Today, as I was nearing the finish line, I thought about him winning with that big smile, as I crossed the line."

"You weren't focused on winning? You were thinking of my dad? That's kind of weird."

"Like I said, I ran a lot of miles and he was with me in spirit for many of them. Its been a journey." Jeff wiped his eyes with the cocktail napkin.

Ellie wiped her eyes with her bar towel.

"The marathon wipes you out and I guess I'm a little emotional as well as exhausted." Jeff folded his hands on the bar.

"It's a good story and you must have run a hell of a race, even if you are a little nuts. Come back when you're home and we'll talk again. I'll keep your medal here in the cup with my dad's. It's a place of honor for our family." She patted his hand.

Jeff's father returned. Ellie disappeared into the kitchen. She returned with the pasta and bread. "Lunch is on the house today boys, in honor of your race and my Dad, Jeff." She left to take care of another table.

"What did I miss? That was very nice of her to buy our lunch."

"I told her about her father, a champion runner and Olympian." Jeff motioned with his pasta spoon towards the picture and trophy.

They finished their meal. Ellie cleared the plates.

"Will I see you again," she asked as they stood, pulling their coats on.

"I hope so. I'll stop by when I'm home for the holidays. I'm going to miss the old ghost." Jeff held up his glass to Bill's picture for the final sip.

****

Jeff stood outside the business school, still in his warm-up gear from the race. It was late, the parking lot mostly empty. Her car was in its normal spot for the top student in finance. A light shone from the student lounge above.

So much had happened since they last talked. Life had moved on and maybe she had too. Jeff entered the building, climbing the steps with some difficulty, the after effects of the race and cramped flight. He reached the second-floor lounge with some effort, focusing on the small figure curled on the sofa, next to a lamp. Books and papers were spread on the table in front of her.

Jeff stood in front of Libby. "Hi." It was a little more than a whisper.

She looked up but was silent. After a few moments, she went back to her book with a barely noticeable exhale of frustration.

"I wanted to see if we could talk. It's been a while."

"Jeff, you've had a month-and-a-half to talk to me." Her face was red, her voice strained, holding back. "We're in the same freaking school, not to mention picking up the fucking phone."

"I'm sorry. I know its no excuse but there were things I needed to clear up." Silence followed. Libby looked away.

After an uncomfortable quiet, she responded. "You chose her over me. That really hurt." She spoke to her book, away from Jeff.

"I'm sorry, Libby. I only stayed a few minutes and I didn't choose her. I chose you, but you'd already left. I had to confront Martine and my feelings. I had to make sure there was nothing there. There wasn't and I walked away. I should have come to find you then."

Libby took a deep breath, looking back to Jeff. "You race today?" He nodded. "Did you win?"

"Third, I made the podium." He grinned, holding up his arms to mount the imaginary dias. He immediately regretted the charade as she rolled her eyes. "I had a good day, a good run, and I got to spend time with my father. That's one of the issues I needed to deal with. There was the school project, being banned from the track team, my parents, and just getting ready to race."

"I saw your presentation. It was really good."

"Thanks. You were there?"

"I sat in the back. Are you taking the internship? I heard about the offer."

"Yes, I think I will."

"I got one, too, with the finance department at Sarah Lee. It's starting, isn't it? Things getting busy and more complicated before we graduate, like you said." Her voice had quieted. She shifted on the couch, loading her books into her bag.

"That's great, Lib. You deserve it. Yeah, I think it will get busier, but that's not a bad thing. It's life. There's one more thing."

"Bill? Your ghost coach. You still think he was real?"

"What's real? I know the workouts I did and the miles I ran were real. I know school and what you and I shared was real." He stopped. "It all sounds so crazy now, doesn't it? But he's gone for good. What happened at the finish was kind of amazing. It's a good story if you're interested."

She stood, pulling on her coat and bag. "Okay. I'm up for a good story."

"Can we go somewhere else? I'll buy. Had a good pay day today."

The two headed down the stairs and outside to the parking lot, stopping by her car. "I'll drive. Get in," she said, opening the car door.

"Where are we going, Penelope's?"

"No, it's late. Lets go to my place." She smiled for the first time. "I bought some dark beer today. It's funny. I bought it because you like it and it reminded me of you. I was standing in the market getting teary over a six pack of beer. I've missed you, shithead." Both laughed, the ice broken.

"You don't mind talking to a slightly salty, tired marathoner?"

"No, I've missed that guy, too. I think you know where the shower is at my place." Libby put her hand on his. "Come over, get cleaned up, then you can tell me all about Baltimore, the finish, and what comes next.

William Agee winning the 1930 Baltimore Marathon.
Used by permission from *The Baltimore Sun*

ACKNOWLEDGMENTS

Much of the inspiration for this book came from the wonderful marathon runners of the 1930's, men largely forgotten today. Clarence DeMar is well known for his Boston Marathon wins and Bronze medal in Paris, in 1924. The 1928 Amsterdam Olympic Marathon team included Joey Ray (5th, 2:36), Albert 'Whitey' Michelson, the former World Record holder (9th, 2:38), DeMar (27th, 2:40), James Hennigan (39th, 2:56), Harvey Frick (41st, 2:57), and William Agee, a colorful and prolific road racer, All-American, and Hall of Famer from Baltimore. After winning the Baltimore trials (there were two other trials held at Boston and Los Angeles), Bill had an off day in Amsterdam, finishing 44th in 2:58.50. These men were very colorful and prolific road racers.

I'd like to thank my friends and teammates from the 1980's at Wake Forest University and the Twin City Track Club in Winston-Salem, North Carolina. Some of you might recognize a similar name, a workout, or race that we ran together. Please know that I enjoyed every step run in your company and hope I represented that era and our time together well. I hope you remember it as fondly as I do.

There were a number of people who helped with the publication of this book. First, the maestro, best-selling author, David L. Robbins. He, more than anyone, helped me hone this story from several lose ideas about my own running experience and the historical characters I'd discovered. I met David after signing up for his Master Writing Class at Virginia Commonwealth

University on a whim. I'd also like to thank my writing group, Jeff Barnes, Pam Webber, Lisa Mistry, and Patrick Fowler. You all were very patient and kind, guiding me, chapter by chapter. Also, my thanks to Lindy Bumgarner for her wonderful web design, and Jessica Capozzola, photography. I'd like to also thank Apprentice House Press for publishing my book, and staff Cara Hullings, my exceptional editor, Miranda Nolan, marketing, and Molly Werts, book design. I am grateful to Apprentice House Press for publishing my story.

I'd also like to thank Mr. Paul McArdell of the Baltimore Sun for his help with articles and pictures of the men from the 1930's. Also, the wonderful reference staff at the Enoch Pratt Library in Baltimore. I'd also like to recognize the great cities of Winston-Salem and Baltimore, and village of Fell's Point for the lovely settings.

I also need to thank my wife and best friend, Wendy; for sticking with me through all the runs and races, and my most recent passion, writing this novel. Your support means everything!

ABOUT THE AUTHOR:

Qualifying for and competing in the 1984 Olympic Marathon Trials was a career highlight in my running journey; a journey that began in junior high and high school as an average, middle-of-the-pack cross country runner. I was fortunate to "walk-on" at East Carolina University, earn a scholarship, and leave with several school records in 1979. From there to Wake Forest University and graduate school, I continued to train and race in the US and abroad in what turned out to be a very competitive time in U.S. road racing in the 1980's. Regrettably, my experience at the Olympic Trials was similar to Jeff Dillon's. I finished in 100th place with a time of 2 hours and 38 minutes, *with much less drama!* As it turned out, the Baltimore Marathon later that year was a highlight and the proverbial comeback race which helped frame this story.

Retirement always follows the athlete too soon. Mine occurred after graduating from Wake Forest in 1985. After a brief but enjoyable Masters campaign in the early 2000's that included a silver medal in the 5000-meters at Sr. Nationals and competing in the 10,000-meters at the Masters World Championships in Puerto Rico; I broke 40-minutes for 10,000-meters one last time at age 50 and hung up my spikes for good. It was a good long run.

Today I enjoy writing, staying fit, and playing golf with friends and family.

Apprentice
House Press
Loyola University Maryland

Apprentice House is the country's only campus-based, student-staffed book publishing company. Directed by professors and industry professionals, it is a nonprofit activity of the Communication Department at Loyola University Maryland.

Using state-of-the-art technology and an experiential learning model of education, Apprentice House publishes books in untraditional ways. This dual responsibility as publishers and educators creates an unprecedented collaborative environment among faculty and students, while teaching tomorrow's editors, designers, and marketers.

Outside of class, progress on book projects is carried forth by the AH Book Publishing Club, a co-curricular campus organization supported by Loyola University Maryland's Office of Student Activities.

Eclectic and provocative, Apprentice House titles intend to entertain as well as spark dialogue on a variety of topics. Financial contributions to sustain the press's work are welcomed. Contributions are tax deductible to the fullest extent allowed by the IRS.

To learn more about Apprentice House books or to obtain submission guidelines, please visit www.apprenticehouse.com.

Apprentice House
Communication Department
Loyola University Maryland
4501 N. Charles Street
Baltimore, MD 21210
Ph: 410-617-5265 • Fax: 410-617-2198
info@apprenticehouse.com • www.apprenticehouse.com

CPSIA information can be obtained
at www.ICGtesting.com
Printed in the USA
BVHW041422031019
560142BV00009B/164/P